I0587238

CALL OF TEMPTATION

CALL OF THE LYCAN

MICHELLE M. PILLOW

MICHELLE M. PILLOW® - MICHELLEPILLOW.COM

Call of Temptation (Call of the Lycan) © Copyright 2008 - 2018, Michelle M. Pillow

Second Print Edition July 2018

First Print Edition September 25, 2017

Second Electronic Printing April 2011

First Electronic Printing January 2008

Published by The Raven Books LLC

ISBN 978-1-62501-195-4

ALL RIGHTS RESERVED.

This book or any portion thereof may not be reproduced or used in any manner whatsoever without the express written permission of the publisher except for the use of brief quotations in a book review.

This novel is a work of fiction. Any and all characters, events, and places are of the author's imagination and should not be confused with fact. Any resemblance to persons, living or dead, or events or places is merely coincidence.

Michelle M. Pillow® is a registered trademark of The Raven Books LLC

James O'Connell lives simply, except for the whole hunting werewolves part. As one of the three lycan princes of the O'Connell clan, it's his duty to enforce the lycan law. When a member of their clan begins killing humans, he's sent to bring the rogue wolf in.

Claudia Hughes lives an ordinary life as a computer software analyst. Her mother and grandmother had psychic intuition, but hers is severely underdeveloped. Taking a solitary vacation, she trusted where instinct led her and ended up at the end of some crazy woman's fangs. She's led into a surreal world where lycans exist and passion for the man who saved her is the least of her worries.

CALL OF THE LYCAN SERIES

Call of the Sea
Call of the Untamed
Call of Temptation

MICHELLE'S BESTSELLING SERIES

QURILIXEN WORLD NOVELS

Dragon Lords Series
Barbarian Prince
Perfect Prince
Dark Prince
Warrior Prince
His Highness The Duke
The Stubborn Lord
The Reluctant Lord
The Impatient Lord
The Dragon's Queen

Lords of the Var® Series
The Savage King

The Playful Prince
The Bound Prince
The Rogue Prince
The Pirate Prince

❖

Captured by a Dragon-Shifter Series
Determined Prince
Rebellious Prince
Stranded with the Cajun
Hunted by the Dragon
Mischievous Prince
Headstrong Prince

❖

Space Lords Series
His Frost Maiden
His Fire Maiden
His Metal Maiden
His Earth Maiden
His Woodland Maiden

❖

Qurilixen Lords Series

Dragon Prince

Marked Prince

More Coming Soon!

To learn more about the Qurilixen World series of
books and to stay up to date on the latest book list
visit www.MichellePillow.com

To stay informed about when a new book in the series installments is released, sign up for updates:

michellepillow.com/author-updates

To my fabulous partner, Mandy M. Roth. Working with you is a real pleasure!

PROLOGUE

Claudia Hughes couldn't help herself as she sang at the top of her lungs. The off-key sound of her voice clashed with the oldies on the radio, but it didn't matter. No one could hear her as she sped down the interstate. Almost longingly, she glanced at her cell phone on the seat next to her, wishing someone would call—even if the only people who'd contact her were coworkers needing help with some software glitches. It wasn't like they knew her anyway. She worked alone for the most part, sitting at home in a pair of exercise pants in front of a computer.

The lonely existence wasn't planned. The town she lived in didn't have any good jobs and the house she owned was paid for, thanks to her mother's will.

Being hired by a firm in nearby Cincinnati had been a lucky break. They didn't even require her to drive in to work.

The East Coast called and she pressed down on the pedal, smiling slightly at the radar detector that kept her from getting pulled over by police. Suddenly, seeing a turn-off for Rhode Island, she took a deep breath. Every time she saw the words *Rhode Island* a tingle worked over her. Without much thought, she followed her gut instinct, knowing it was what her mother and grandmother would have told her to do. Making her tires screech, she swerved to make the exit.

Rhode Island had never been in the plan, but she knew she had to trust her instincts. Her psychic abilities might not be as strong as her mother's had been, but she knew she had to trust them. Something important awaited her at the end of this journey and she would keep driving until she found it.

Grabbing her sunglasses off the seat, she slipped them on and rolled down her window to let the cooling breeze in. Destiny was out there and she was going to find it.

2

"WHERE IS THAT BITCH?" James O'Connell frowned, narrowing his eyes as he scanned the long balcony overlooking the sea. He breathed hard, sniffing the air as the full moon threatened him with a shift. Being a natural-born lycanthrope, he was ruled by the full moon but not controlled by it. More than that, he was called to the sea, for the moon controlled the tides just as it controlled the stirring of his blood. The sensation of power was like a drug and it caused many of his kind to live by the water.

His senses enhanced by the nature around him, he scanned the shadows along the wooden deck. A crisp breeze came off the Atlantic Ocean, stinging his nose as he tried to pick up on Meghan's elusive scent. Under his breath, he swore in frustration, "Fuck!"

He couldn't have lost her again, not after finally tracking her down on the somewhat remote island twelve miles off Rhode Island's mainland. Luckily for him, Meghan wasn't exactly the "camping-out" type and he didn't have to search the seventeen miles of shoreline to find her. All he had to do was go to the fanciest hotels and resorts on the island until someone recognized her photograph. It didn't take long. With Meghan's jet-black hair, tanned skin, generous breasts and penchant for wearing revealing clothing, she stood out in a crowd of humans like a walking goddess. Too bad this goddess was deadly.

Thinking to catch the barest hint of her scent, he began jogging along the deck. The beast lurking within him was fierce and always ready to unleash itself, but it was worse on the full moon, it was worse when it came to hunting Meghan. The bitch had nearly killed his oldest brother, Ian, future king of the O'Connell clan, and Ian's sea-swept bride, Ceana.

Technically, Ian was next in line to rule upon the death of the lycan king, their father, then James and finally the youngest, Roark. But, since they were immortal, unless some horrific event occurred, it was unlikely that any of the brothers would ever rule. James was fine with that. He would much rather have his family than a crown.

Roark, like James, had his own duties to the lycan clan. They were hunters, bringing justice to the rogue wolves—like Meghan—who broke their laws, meager laws that they were. She had betrayed the clan and tried to kill Ian when the oldest O'Connell didn't choose her as his bride and future queen. Though Ian and Meghan had a century-long affair of the flesh, James was very glad to know Ian hadn't tricked himself into thinking he loved Meghan. The bitch would no doubt have plotted to kill the king if she'd been next in line for the throne.

Meghan's crimes didn't end with her betrayal. After the assassination attempt, she had laid low for a while, ending up in Las Vegas where James was first able to track her down. Only after getting there did he realize she'd been a busy little lycan. She'd been killing showgirls and leaving their mutilated corpses in dark alleyways, as if taunting him with her misdeeds. When James got near and stopped her game, she'd been livid. Meghan had gone on a killing rampage, leaving a trail of human female corpses across Nevada, Idaho, Oregon and Washington. Some in the clan believed she'd gone up to Canada, but in truth, she'd merely tried to throw them off her scent, becoming more discreet about hiding her victims' bodies, as she turned her attention south, zigzagging a haphazard pattern across the United States.

Feasting on mortals was forbidden. It was one of the oldest of their laws. Lycans were an ancient people, their race as old as the humans', growing with the humans from a time when mortals knew of all the supernatural races. They used to be hunted, condemned as evil by the church. Sure, times were wilder in the early days, but so it was with all the races—mortal and supernatural. Just as humans no longer roamed the countryside pillaging and wielding swords so did his people no longer uncontrollably wield claw and fang.

In present times, humans denied their existence, which suited most of the supernaturals just fine. But their denial led them in circles when it came to Meghan, searching for a killer who could not be caught by their mortal means. With Roark newly married, it was up to James to find Meghan and punish her. It was a task that weighed heavily upon him, as she was proving to be a cunning adversary. And with each new victim, she seemed to grow stronger and more elusive.

Lucky for all, her killings had yet to result in a human being turned. Death came much easier to mortals than a changing. Not only would it be an embarrassment for the clan, since James was expected to prevent such a thing, it would be another burden James did not need—taking care of a young one. Circumstances had to be right, the bloodline perfect and the moon full for the bite to take effect. It fell into natural order that if attacking humans was against the law, so was trying to turn them. A lycan could attack fifty mortals and possibly only one would start to turn. Reason dictated that if one was turned, the odds were that many had been attacked. Even then it didn't guarantee the mortal would make it through the horrifically painful process.

"Fucking cunt!" James leapt over the stairs leading down to the sandy beach. The slippery footing didn't halt his progress as he sprinted along the shore. Stars spread out, punctuating the cloudless sky. Despite the cold sea air, that really didn't bother him, it was a perfect night. He would have preferred rain, as the foul weather would surely keep humans indoors. Though the beach appeared abandoned where he was, he could detect human voices in the distance. It prevented him from shifting and catching Meghan all the faster.

"No," a breathy whisper caught his attention. He started to ignore it as he filtered through the voices to find Meghan, but something in the way the word trembled kept his attention. "Get off me!"

James focused his thoughts, not breaking stride. The sounds of a struggle ensued, the unmistakable sounds of a fight. Light grunts pitted against an evil laugh. He'd been around too long not to recognize what happened. A mortal woman was caught in Meghan's grasp and, by the sound of it, she was putting up one hell of a fight. Amazement filled him at the mortal's stamina. Not many could stand up to a lycan, especially when being attacked.

"Ouch!" Meghan's voice swore. A loud smack followed the word. "You stupid, fucking cunt, you broke my rib! Oh, that's it. Playtime is over, you mortal piece of shit."

Meghan! James yelled, directing his thoughts toward the lycan woman. He used the telepathic link lycans shared to yell at her. *Stop!*

"Stay back." The woman's yell sounded closer than before, but it was still a long run down the beach. It was only by focusing his lycan hearing that he managed to catch the words. James shivered at the soft quality to her voice, even as she yelled at her attacker. The blood pumping in his veins made it easy for his cock to stir at the sound. "I don't know what you want or who you think you are, lady, but I don't want to have to hurt you."

"You, hurt me?" Meghan laughed harder.

"I will if I have to. I know how to defend myself. Just walk away," Meghan's victim answered.

Again James was amazed that the woman stood up to a lycan. He could detect Meghan's anger by the way her loud breath pierced the night. Mortals would not be able to detect the sound but he could with his enhanced hearing.

You have a choice, James. Save the girl or catch the queen. Meghan's voice whispered through his thoughts. *I admit, I wonder which you will try to do.*

Meghan! James warned.

"What's wrong with your face?" the mortal asked, gasping. "What are you?"

"I'm your queen, bitch! Bow down to me!" Meghan yelled. James could hear her leaping into the air, heard the soft thud of her body hitting flesh and imagined the piercing of Meghan's fangs into a tender throat. James ran harder. He had to be close now.

"Stop, please...*ow*." The woman's words lost some of the fight.

Meghan! What are you doing? he demanded.

Leave the mortal be and come with me. I swear, if you do, justice will be met.

Justice? Meghan spat out. *You mean your justice, not mine. What justice is there in denying our inner natures? I had forgotten how freeing it is to drink of blood and partake of sex as I see fit. Why do we deny ourselves our birthright? Why suffer ourselves to save mortal sheep? When I want to fuck, I find a hard cock and fuck—whether the man be willing or not. When I wish to drink, I take my drink where I please, from the neck of whichever sweet, young beauty captures my notice. I'm growing more powerful, James, and I'll keep killing so long as you chase me. You won't stop me. No one will stop me and, someday, I will have my own clan, my own warriors underneath my rule and there will be a great war between us, the naturals who do what we were always meant to and you unnaturals who would deny lycan nature and live the lives of monks.*

You will kill if I don't stop you. James ran faster, instinctively going where the mind-link grew stronger.

True, but this way it's your fault another pretty, young mortal will die. She laughed. *Mmm, why must we always fight, James? All these centuries and you've never liked me. Why is that, James? Is it because I fucked your brother and not you? Is it jealousy? I'll admit I miss the strength of a good lycan prince's cock. How about it? Will you shift and fuck me, James? How long has it been since you've ridden a real lycan woman? How long since you've ridden anything at all? Perhaps you like being a monk.*

James hated how his cock instantly lifted at her words, pressing hard against his stiff denim jeans. It had indeed been a long time since he'd felt the soft velvet of a pussy squeezing him, and the combination of the hunt, the moon and the ocean only urged the primal, instinctive lusts to course through his blood.

Was that a moan of interest, James? Even in his head, Meghan's voice was thick and sultry. *Should we call a truce just for tonight? I can let this one go. She's weak but she might live yet if I let her go now. Would you do it, James? Would you fuck me to save this one's life? How about later? Would you be my king and fuck me every night, James? Would you spray your hot cum all over my big breasts? In my hot, wet pussy? In my tight, luscious ass?*

James nearly howled at the imagery. He hated Meghan with more passion than anything else in his immortal life, and yet she knew how to tempt their kind, knew what to say, how to send images of her words into his mind. A flash of a tanned ass, cheeks spread, came into his mind, the tight rosette right there as if waiting to be taken.

Or would you prefer my mouth, James? The words purred and whined at the same time, followed by the image of perfect bowed lips around a thick lycan cock. *Should I suck the poison from your thick wound? Would you like that, James? Would you like to punish me for my crimes with your big, hard, thick, pounding sword? You could take me here, on the beach with the smell of the ocean and this mortal's blood in our noses. I feel the beast in you, it's the same one I carry. The beast is thirsty. He wants a drink, doesn't he, James? I won't tell anyone if you indulge this one, little time. Promise.*

Finally he detected Meghan with his eyes. She stood in the distance but he saw her easily with his naturally enhanced vision. Her breast was pulled from her dress's floral bodice, hanging naked and free in the night air.

Pinching a nipple, she moaned. *What is your answer, James? Will you fuck me to save her life? Will you dip your prick into the very thing you hate to save this one, simple, disgusting mortal?*

James bit his lip hard with a growing fang, drawing blood. His eyes focused on the woman's breast, ignoring the fallen human lying in the sand next to her. For the briefest of moments, he considered Meghan's words. Whatever fight the mortal had put up was gone now. As he drew nearer, he saw Meghan's hand was covered in blood and she rubbed the dark fluid on her breast. His inner beast tried to rise up. Everything about Meghan disgusted him.

Meghan's eyes flashed with golden promise. She touched the flowing skirt, tugging it up to reveal her perfect thighs. The smell of blood and feminine desire assaulted his nostrils. This was not a plan of attack he'd been ready for.

Yes, he growled at her, hoping she wouldn't sense his distaste for her, hoping she'd mistake the gruffness of his thoughts as desire and not repulsion. If he had to fuck Meghan to save the mortal, he would. *Give me your word that you will let her live and I will fuck you.*

Really? she purred, pulling her skirt higher to reveal she wore no panties over her clean-shaven pussy. *Right here?*

Yes, he answered her breathy plea, refusing to look at what she showed him. *Get on your knees for me.*

Meghan laughed, her tone cruel. She sunk to her knees in the sand. He was close now, so close. His heart thumped heavily, blocking out all but her words.

Instead of doing as he commanded, she reached for the half-dead woman next to her. Pulling the frail human by the arm, Meghan grinned at him, her eyes flashing deadly as she bared her fangs. Without pause, she sunk them into the human's throat, drinking noisily so James could hear each suckle. Meghan's laughter filled him, mocking him, scorning him.

Sorry, lover boy, but you're not lycan enough to ride me, Meghan taunted, even as she drank. Then, letting the woman's body fall onto the ground, she stood, smiling evilly. Blood covered her lips but did not drip down her throat, showing how delicately she had drunk. She yelled over the beach, "But now you can eternally carry the guilt of knowing you would have succumbed to me, James, just as you will carry the knowledge that you will never catch me. You have failed everyone you love. You have failed your family and your clan. You are no match for a true lycan queen. You are pathetic!"

Meghan darted toward the water, to the lapping waves that ate at the shore. James shifted direction as the sound of an engine punctured the night. He'd been so caught up hiding his disgust, he hadn't seen the small fishing vessel drifting close to the shore, nor detected the lycan who'd been waiting patiently along the bottom of the boat. Laughter filled his head as Meghan splashed through the water to reach the vessel. She leapt from the waves, landing neatly inside. Instantly the boat moved, slicing forward through the water toward the mainland.

James howled in frustration, loud and long, as the boat carried her away. He could not swim to catch her, not twelve miles, not through the deep ocean waters and thick currents. His only hope was to steal a boat of his own or catch a ferry to the mainland in the morning, as the last ferry he had debarked from this Friday evening had already left at 8:15. He knew, because he'd meticulously checked the schedules.

Before he could steal a boat, he had to dispose of the human woman's body. A pang of sorrow filled him as he remembered her voice, how she'd fought to live. He couldn't leave her with perfect puncture wounds on her neck, not if he hoped this attack would be blamed on some wild dog. Blood pumped in his veins, still raging from Meghan's taunts. Though the lycan bitch could never tempt him, he hated himself for letting her think she had. He cursed her for attempting to penetrate him in such a way, trying to turn his inborn weaknesses against him —desire, blood, the moon and ocean. They were a heady combination any lycan male would fall for. She knew he could not let a mortal die, not when he could stop it. She knew she could force him to fuck her if he thought it would save a life—no matter how he loathed the very idea of it.

But he wasn't just any lycan male. He was James O'Connell, prince of the O'Connell clan, hunter, defender of the laws. He could not afford to fail. Yet, he had. He'd fallen for the hope that he could stop her, could save this one human. And now Meghan had eluded him again. How many more humans would she kill because he'd tried to save one?

"Don't be so noble, James," he told himself, struggling to put the fire in his belly out. "Meghan was right, you are pathetic."

As he turned to see what his failed attempt had awarded him, his gaze fell upon the unmoving figure on the ground. Like the others, she was pretty and slender, her skin pale from lack of blood. Long brown hair covered her face from view, tousled from the way she'd been dropped unceremoniously to the sand. The locks shone in soft, gentle curls, nearly gleaming in the moonlight. Her petite frame would hardly have given much of a fight to one as strong and determined as Meghan.

Blood stained her navy and light blue silk blouse, ruining the fine material. Drawstrings hung along her arms, winding like snakes over her still flesh. Though meant to be loose, the shirt clung to her curves. Too bad he had been too late.

Gently, even though he knew she could no longer feel it, he reached to scoop her into his arms. At his touch, the corpse gasped, shivering violently. Startled, James dropped his hold. The woman convulsed upon the ground as her body was racked with terrible pain. She cried out.

"No," James shook his head, trying to will what was happening to stop. "Die, just die. Don't fight death. The pain that awaits you will only last. Welcome the peace that comes. Don't fight to live."

The woman screamed again and he knew she wasn't listening. Her body did what bodies instinctively did—it fought to survive. Only this was most likely to be a losing battle. James swore under his breath, glancing out at the ocean to where Meghan's boat had disappeared. He couldn't steal a boat and give chase, not now, not when there was a changing human he needed to take care of. There were no others on the island to leave her with.

Almost calculatingly, he again looked at the woman writhing in agony. Yet, if by some miracle she lived, she might be the key to stopping Meghan. Her tie to the treacherous bitch would be strong. Turned ones always sought those who killed them. It was a strange irony that they'd be drawn to the makers of their mortal deaths.

Having had more training with turned humans over the centuries than he'd like to admit, James cleared his throat and reached for the woman's face. His fingers tangled in her soft hair before finding her sand-covered cheek. Emotions whirled inside him as he looked at the woman, compassion and pity, curiosity and a sense of duty and honor. Brushing the locks from her features, he revealed a pretty, little mouth and big, scared, dark eyes.

James took a deep breath, the words of comfort he planned on uttering leaving him completely as he stared. Her lips opened wide and she gasped for breath, but she no longer screamed. Ocean waves crashed near them, pulling and pushing his soul with each surging of the tide.

"You," she whispered, almost accusatorily. "My ancestors whispered to me in my dreams that I would find you." She closed her eyes tight and the strange spell between them dissipated as she again began to yell in pain. Her words made no sense and he knew the loss of blood had made her delirious.

"Easy, young one, I will care for you. Let the pain lead you into darkness. Once you pass out, it will be easier to bear." James lifted her into his arms, scanning the beach to see if anyone was near. If she kept screaming, she'd draw attention and the last thing he wanted was some do-gooder coming to her rescue. Careful not to suffocate her, he smothered her face into his chest, letting the vibrations of her torment muffle against him. Her light body barely slowed down his steps as he jogged with her across the shore, back toward the small inn where he'd procured a suite earlier.

When he saw a group of people walking and laughing along the shoreline, a strained smile came to his lips and he gripped the woman in his arms tighter to silence her cries. He veered away from the group, hoping the meager distance would afford him safe passage. Their attention turned briefly to them and he smiled, trying to force all the charm and ease his tight, stressed body could manage. One of the men, a yuppie in white slacks and a blue polo shirt, waved.

"I see someone has had too much to drink," a woman exclaimed merrily. The others laughed, resuming their conversation. The woman in his arms pushed hard against him and managed to free her head. She opened her mouth, ready to yell. James crushed his lips down on hers, taking her would-be scream into his mouth. The woman jolted, her mouth jerking against him, more from the writhing in her body than any measured response. Still, the kiss startled him with the intense lust it conjured. James gripped her tighter, pried his mouth away before he delved his tongue again into the warm depths. He sighed in mild relief when he made it past the group of humans. He pressed her face to his chest once more.

By small degrees, the woman's cries lessened, as did her struggling. His rented quarters were right off the beach, reached by a small, worn trail in the surrounding narrow strip of tall grasses. The company had called it a suite but it was really more like a private building isolated from other guests. It was the only lodging available on the island due to tourist season and he was suddenly glad that luck had afforded him privacy and two bedrooms—not that they would be staying there long.

As he carried the woman up the narrow, wooden stairs to the deck, the sound of faraway music from a dockside restaurant penetrated his thoughts. In any other situation, carrying a woman to his ocean-side bedroom, surrounded by soft music and moonlight, would have been highly romantic. Finally reaching the sliding glass door, he set the woman's feet on the ground. Her head lulled back and she whimpered.

Pulling the key from his pocket, he unlocked the door and once more picked her up to carry her inside. A queen-size bed, television and small chair were the only amenities in the bedroom besides the faux-oak dressers. Laying her gingerly on the bed, he moved to shut the door in case she began screaming again. Moonlight streamed through the room and he quickly pulled the curtains shut, blocking it out. The darkness didn't bother him as he navigated the room with ease. Walking to the large bathroom adjoining his room, he flipped on the light. A soft glow illuminated the bed, as if framing her for his perusal.

With time to study her, he strode slowly across the floor, watching his shadow move over her body. Putting one knee on the bed, he leaned over her, telling himself he was just checking her vitals. But instead of her heartbeat, he listened to her raspy, almost passionate-sounding breath. Instead of gauging her temperature, his fingers caressed her soft skin, brushing granules of sand from her cheek and jaw. He pushed back her hair, revealing the bite mark on her neck. About a half-dozen puncture marks indented her flesh, attesting to Meghan's bites. The smell of blood wafted up to him, her blood.

A moan filtered past his lips as he instinctively leaned closer. Drawing his tongue along her throat, he licked, stroking long and slow over her flesh. A thready pulse caught up in his ears as the taste of her essence filled him. The memory of the forced kiss on the beach made his lips tingle. Unable to help himself, he did it again, moving his mouth to her still one. It had been decades since he'd tasted human blood and the salty tang was just as sweet and pleasurable as he remembered. His lips slid back to her throat, tasting her. The beast inside him howled in ecstasy until James too gave a light howl of approval. His lust hit him hard.

The woman jerked, her hand weakly hitting his head. "No," she whimpered, as if that was all the fight she had left in her.

The word penetrated his passion-hazed mind and he drew back, panting hard and heavy. He'd only had the smallest taste of her and already his cock was nearly exploding in his pants. He needed release, wanted to find it in her delicate body, but he knew he could never act like such a monster. He began to speak but her mouth stopped him. She moaned softly, turning her lips to his as if searching for his kiss. This time, she moved them, opening her mouth as if to receive him.

James jerked violently as he tried to resist, but even as he braced his arms to pull back, he found his tongue pushing forward, testing the wet resolve of her mouth as his cock wished to test her pussy. He drew his tongue in and out in a slow, steady rhythm, slipping by her lips each time she tried to close around him in a kiss. The feel was pure, agonizing torment.

"I want to fuck you," he whispered into her mouth, without thought or reason. "I want to sink my cock deep inside you and ride you until you can't stand."

"Ah," she whimpered.

James drew back, realizing what he'd said to her. He sobered. This wasn't some kind of seduction where he was supposed to talk dirty to arouse his partner. No, this was a human turning into one of his kind. What was wrong with him? Had Meghan's words aroused him to the point of insanity? Or was it this female? Her scent? Her blood? The soft, silk-covered breast that had somehow worked its way beneath his strong fingers?

With a low sound of torment, he pushed himself from the bed, turning toward the light in an effort to put distance between them. But the door to the bathroom made a poor barrier as he slammed it shut. Catching himself in the mirror, he met his reflected gaze. Yellow glinted in his dark brown eyes, framed by the wild mess of his chin-length brown hair. Parting his lips, he saw his fangs protruding from his gums.

Almost desperately, he gripped the knobs of the shower, turning it on. He clawed at his black t-shirt, tearing it from his muscled chest. His long nails sliced into his skin, but the tiny bit of pain only added to his lustful state. Finally free of the shirt, he threw it at the big tub on a platform on the far side of the bathroom. Steam flooded the room from the running water. James gingerly unbuttoned his tight pants, wanting to scream at the sensitive pain each bump of his hard cock caused him. The taut flesh nearly throbbed for attention and he found himself stepping into the scalding-hot shower before his pants even fell from his hips. The blood from his chest washed away as the wounds he'd made healed.

Water soaked into his sneakers and weighed the denim as he pushed it down, off his thighs. Leaning against the wall, unfazed by the extreme heat of the water, he took himself in hand. Groaning, he stroked his long cock with the aid of the water, letting his fist slide up and down. With each stroke, he squeezed, still tasting the stranger's blood in his mouth. Even as his hand brought pleasure, he wanted more, he wanted lips sucking, he wanted a tight pussy clamping down on him, he wanted to taste more blood.

Gripping his shaft with both hands, he began working himself hard, almost painfully thrusting his fists up and down, up and down. His balls ached but he didn't have a hand to spare for them as he tried to milk the cum from the mushroomed tip of his dick.

"Come on, come on," he growled, unmindful of how loud the words might be. Suddenly he smelled her—the woman in his bed. His senses were sharp, heightened in his aroused state. The memory pushed him on and he frantically rocked his hips. He remembered the softness of her silk-covered breast, wishing he could have torn the shirt just a little to get a peek at her nipples. Just the idea of seeing her naked was enough to finally push him over the edge. The climax hit him hard as a thick stream of cum jetted onto the shower wall. "*Ah-ahha.*"

A sharp intake of breath assaulted his ears and he stiffened. Reaching for the curtain, he pulled it aside. The woman stood in his bathroom, her brown eyes wide as she stared at him. The steam from the shower dampened her shirt, causing it to cling to her breasts and stomach until he could see every lacy detail of the bra underneath. Her gaze traveled down to where one of his hands still wrapped his somewhat limber cock.

His words hoarse, he demanded, "How come you are awake? It's impossible. You shouldn't be able to move for weeks."

Claudia trembled, her body weak and her mind hazy. She wasn't sure what had awoken her from her burning, pain-filled dreams, but she was drawn to the door next to the bed. Steam rolled through the gap and light showed from the other side. When she opened the door, there was a blast of heat but the low groans she heard made her stiffen to her spot on the floor.

Then, suddenly, the curtain was pulled away and the most handsome man she'd ever seen stood before her, pants around his ankles, cock firmly in hand. There was something familiar about him. He reminded her of a hazy premonition she'd received but couldn't understand. Her grandmother had been a psychic, so had her mother, but Claudia's gifts had never fully developed despite her family's early efforts to train her. All she got were impressions, images and feelings—like the one that had made her change her vacation plans mid-drive, taking her to Block Island instead of Maine. The particular premonition that included this man had come in the form of a dream and was about as clear as standing nose to canvas in front of an Impressionist painting, fuzzy and lacking the subtle details of the bigger picture. It was more of a feeling, an idea, an innate knowledge that would someday be made clear.

Stunned, she swallowed, noticing how the motion only made the pain in her throat worse. Her memory of the night was a cloudy haze and she tried to grasp for details. She knew she couldn't be drunk, because she didn't drink, and she couldn't be drugged, because she didn't do drugs and the only dinner she'd had was off a salad bar.

"How come you are awake? It's impossible. You shouldn't be able to move for weeks," he said. The words, low and dark and so very final, made her shiver in apprehension.

"I don't feel well. What's happening to me?" Her gaze moved back to his face, though it was hard to pry her attention from the enormous shaft in his hands. She silently pleaded for answers with her eyes, unsure as to what she wanted.

"You've been attacked and bitten in the neck. I've brought you to someplace safe. You have nothing to fear from me."

The low tone of his raspy voice drew her forward. Her eyes narrowed as she saw his hand grip tightly around his still semi-erect cock. The bathroom smelled of sex. Her pussy clenched at the thought and she stepped forward as if led by a powerful will outside her own. Hot water hit his skin and the fist around his cock pumped slowly at her advance.

"You should go lie down." Though he said the words, they didn't sound convincing. Her mind disregarded them. The lust pouring through her was more powerful than anything she'd ever felt, adding a strange energy and strength that should not have been there. It filled her with euphoria and made her feel as if she could jump off a balcony and fly. Her clit ached, a suddenly tight mass of nerves screaming for attention.

A dream, her mind whispered, easily accepting the explanation. *This has to be a dream.*

"What are you doing?" he asked, studying her face.

Claudia couldn't help the small smile as her primal instincts took over. She pulled at her silk shirt, hearing it rip as she tossed it aside. Her bra was next, followed by her shoes, pants and panties. The man in the shower began to stroke himself to full force, his eyes appearing to glow as he looked at her naked chest.

When she stepped into the shower, the hot water hit her skin, burning as she got used to the heat. Her nipples puckered and she breathed heavily as if she'd run for miles only to end up naked in this man's shower. He continued to stroke his cock and she reached forward, wondering if he'd disappear once she touched him. Her hand met thick, turgid flesh and he nearly howled. She mimicked his movements, gripping him tight as she explored his length. It was unlike anything she'd ever seen or felt, the kind of weapon made for fucking.

Her pussy flooded with cream and the man's nostrils flared. Visions of being pounded into submission against the shower wall flooded her mind. The shower curtain was still open and water sprinkled out onto the floor to create a messy puddle.

Her throat ached and her mouth was dry so she

opened her lips wide. Without thought, she sunk to her knees before him to drink the water from his cock. Heat met her lips and she began to suck the liquid, swallowing it as she did so.

"Ah," the man gasped. His hands gripped her arms tight, but she wasn't sure if he was pulling her off or keeping her on. "Shit."

She glanced up his tight, perfect body and released her mouth's hold. He didn't stop her from standing. Facing him, her eyes wide, she whispered, "Fuck me already."

❖

JAMES SWALLOWED, knowing her sudden, intense passion for him was because of her condition. Only, she shouldn't be awake and experiencing this level of aggression and excitement for another two weeks at the earliest. She should be near-dead, lifeless and pale from being drained of blood. Instead she acted unlike any woman—lycan or mortal—he'd ever seen. She was like a drugged beast, breathing hard and loud.

Their deep lust was why his kind didn't mate with humans. Mortals were too frail, unable to take the full passion. Sure, they slept with them—very cautiously—even dated them. Some lycans even spent lifetimes with mortals but they didn't life-mate permanently with them. Only other immortal supernaturals were suitable life-mates. Too many lycans had seen their human loved ones die as they tried to turn them. It was a painful memory that would be carried into eternity. For, if not killed, the lycan would live forever.

The sweet smell of her sex filled him and he knew he should stop her, tie her up and keep her safe from herself and from him. But the wolf inside him wanted her. *He* wanted her and he didn't have the willpower to pull away to do what he should.

"Fuck me," she commanded, irritation shooting from her lovely eyes.

James took hold of her arms and pressed her against the hard shower wall. Primitive noises escaped him as he frantically worked his hand down to feel the warmth of her pussy. He persuasively grabbed her by the hips, pressing his cock tightly against her moist folds. He massaged and stimulated her clit with his fingers while he wet his shaft in the cream flowing from her sex. She gasped and arched her back, trembling violently with each press.

"You're so hot," she panted, rolling her hips in tiny circles. "Oh, that feels good, just like that."

James growled his response. It took all his willpower to keep the glow from his eyes and his growing fangs hidden. His cock thickened with each thrust against her. Every fiber of him ached to delve inside the sweetness of her cunt.

"Tell me to stop," he ordered, though no part of him wanted her to.

"Ah," she answered.

"You are ill, you're not yourself." He tried to pull his body away, but his hips wouldn't obey as they kept rocking along her slit. If merely rubbing was already heaven, what would happen if he pressed inside? Felt the tight fit of her pussy squeezing him? Stretching for him? Taking him deeper than she'd ever taken any man? His flesh tingled and burned, practically begging him to shift. But he couldn't. To take her as the beast would certainly kill her. Lycans were lusty creatures and, when shifted, they could mindlessly crave both blood and sex, if not carefully managed.

She wasn't one of them yet, might never be. He had to slow himself, needed to draw back before he hurt her. To do that, he needed to hear her protests. If only she'd tell him to stop, that she didn't want this as badly as he, then he could draw back.

Instead she grabbed his face in her hands and

forced his mouth down to hers. Her tongue instantly pushed between his lips in a hard, deep kiss. She rubbed her body against him, her breasts caressing his chest with the aid of the water.

"Ah," she panted, over and over, the sounds growing in strength with each passing moment, "ah... oh...mmh."

She began to shake, her body tightening as she came from the stimulation against her clit. Warmth flooded him and he couldn't deny himself. James lifted her hips, pressing her up against the wall. She was so light. Reaching between them to guide his cock to enter her, she pulled him to probe her tight pussy. He knew, as a mortal, she'd be tight, but the almost-painful squeeze as he dipped the head of his shaft inside her channel was almost too much.

James stared at her lush, full lips as they quivered with soundless pleas. He slipped a little deeper, groaning.

"Ah, it's so big," she gasped.

He pushed deeper still, easing her to his size. He had often prided himself on the strength of his manhood, his enormous cock that drove lycan women and the few humans he'd been with wild, but suddenly it felt more like a curse as he was torn between hurting her and finding his own greedy pleasure.

"That's it," he whispered, trying to coax her. Her small protest was coming way too late. He was too far gone to stop now. He kept her body held up, watching the shifting muscles of her face as she closed her eyes tight. Her legs moved restlessly against his hips, tightening and releasing their hold, torn between opening wider and closing.

The sweet, fresh scent of her natural perfume teased his senses. He tried to make his lips move into a comforting smile, but the look had to be strained. Her smell was too much to resist. "Rub your clit. Make your pussy wetter."

She reached between their bodies, finding the hard pearl of her clit. Rubbing it in slow circles, she grunted and James reveled in the feel of the sweet release of cream on his cock. He thrust, deep and sure, seating himself nearly to the brink. She gasped, stiffening against him.

"Ah, there it is. You feel so good, *a thaisce*—my treasure." He pulled out slightly, keeping his movements slow and shallow.

She gave a light moan, stimulating her clit as he eased himself in and out. James bit his lip, keeping the dirty thoughts he was having inside his brain. He had no wish to scare her with the things he wanted to do to her. A part of his mind told him this was wrong, to stop, that she wasn't in a state to make such a decision, but the glide of her sex argued the fact, told him she wanted it.

"Fuck...me...harder," she ground out as if possessed.

He had to obey. The beast in him was too close to the surface. The full moon, the close waves, the rampant smell of blood and sex was too much for even the most stoic of lycans to fight. He began pounding his hips into her, fucking her hard against the shower wall, mindless as to whether or not he was hurting her. All he knew was the tight fit on his cock, the need for release, the slickness of her wet pussy.

He rammed his hips into her, thumping her back against the shower wall as he braced his legs. His body began to shift, his cock strong as the wolf threatened to emerge. For a moment, he felt himself slipping into her thoughts, his mind trying to connect to her. He resisted, not wanting to violate her thoughts and refusing to read what he did see of them. Her eyes were closed tight, her hands moving to his shoulders as he pumped his hips.

His legs started to break, narrowing as they shifted and grew fur. He grunted loud and hard, trying to keep the beast down so she wouldn't see it. His cock filled out even more and fur tickled his back. Doing the only thing he could think of, he pounded her harder to keep her from focusing her eyes on him. Fangs grew from his mouth and his nose elongated. James put his face in her hair, tempted to bite her but he was held back by the memory that she should have been near death. He kept his face hidden and his grunts loud so she wouldn't see or hear the changes in him.

"Ah!" the woman screamed. Her body clamped his as she came. Her nails bit into his shoulders, drawing blood. Seconds later, he jerked, squirting hot semen as he continued thrusting inside her. When he'd finished, the beast was sated enough to be forced deep inside and the man James could regain complete control. He cleared his throat, awkwardly loud to hide the sound of his breaking legs returning to his human form. Fur pulled inward, replaced by flesh. Remorse for his rough handling surfaced and he was grateful she had not detected his partial shift in her excited state. He let her slide down to her feet. She pushed at him lightly, stumbling from the shower and nearly slipping on the wet floor. Wet hair stuck to her face and neck and she reached to feel the bumpy texture of the wound Meghan had left on her.

Her eyes met his, hazy now and deeply confused. Slowly she stepped back, moving away from the shower stall and into the bedroom. With the lust gone, her body suddenly weakened and, when her knees hit the back of the bed, she instantly fell backward onto the soft mattress. Her eyes closed before her head even landed.

4

"AM I DRINKING TO YOUR SUCCESS?" The king's voice came through the phone. James could picture the look on his father's face without even seeing it. He was hopeful of good news and confident that his son would give it to him.

"No, sorry, Father, you're not." James glanced at the bed, trying not to feel guilty for what he'd done. "Something has happened."

"Meghan has killed again, hasn't she?" Instantly the king's voice dropped in regret.

"Not exactly. She tried but..." James again looked at the woman on the bed. Her legs hung over the sides, just where she'd fallen twenty minutes ago, only now the blanket he'd put over her covered her nudity. He hadn't wanted to touch her, even to move

39

her. He didn't trust himself to act the gentleman, especially now that her husky voice was in his thoughts and the feel of her body emblazoned on his flesh, adding to his quickly growing fascination with her. After he'd stepped from the shower and discarded their torn clothes, he'd towel-dried and slipped into a pair of workout pants and a white t-shirt. It had taken him some time to call his father with the bad news. "The woman Meghan tried to kill is here, in my room."

"You saved her victim? Well done, son! What do you need? Is the human aware of what happened? It will be unfortunate but hopefully she will be convinced otherwise—"

"No, I was too late," James broke in.

"Then..." the king's voice trailed off. A long pause broke their conversation. Finally the king continued, "Will she survive the changing?"

"You know as well as I there is no way to tell this early." James again looked at the woman. Though he was fairly certain she couldn't hear him, he walked toward the balcony door and went outside. The cool breeze stirred his damp hair, giving an even deeper chill to the night. As a lycan, James could easily ignore cold, just as he did the heat. "I think it's time to send backup. Meghan's been feeding, perhaps much more than we know about. She grows strong and overconfident. I would have captured her, if not for the human woman's presence." James quickly told his father of Meghan's plans, of her ranting about being queen of her own "natural" clan, of how she planned to solicit warriors to her rule and wield her power once she got it. He made sure to leave out the part about her seduction attempt. He wouldn't further disgrace himself by admitting he'd verbally given in to the treacherous bitch, even if it was to save a mortal's life.

"Do you think she's serious?" the king asked.

"Someone helped her tonight, a lycan. I think it might have been one of the disbanded Douglass clan, but I can't be sure. I haven't seen them for centuries. I honestly don't remember how strong their numbers were. But I fear if it is them then Meghan will try to bring them together. Without a solid leader, the Douglass clan members might agree to follow her. We know how persuasive she can be." James sighed. "If we can't catch Meghan soon, all the clans should be notified. They won't be happy and I'm afraid of how this will reflect upon our family."

"I'm contacting your brothers. Ian's overseas in India with his wife so it might take me a few days to track him down. Roark and Natasha are at some

Farfadet family gathering. He should be back soon. I'd prefer to keep this in our family for now but, if the other clan elders need to be contacted, I know how to reach them. All can be in the US within a day's notice."

With modern transportation, it was no longer necessary for the clan to live close together, unlike in the old days when they'd have to be able to reach each other on foot in a single night or be close enough to use telepathy. Just like with speech, the farther apart two lycans were, the harder it was to hear each other's thoughts—though telepathy did reach a lot farther than sound.

His father continued, "Until then watch over the young one. She is our responsibility now."

"Can't you send someone to take over her care? Perhaps one of the women? Maybe Giselle? She has a light touch. Or Bridget?"

"You know as well as I that you are the best suited for her care." The king's tone changed ever-so slightly. "You have a way about you, my son, that makes you particularly adept at helping the newly turned to cope with their gifts. There is something about you that the young ones respond to."

"That doesn't mean I'm the only one who can. It's been a very long time since one was turned,"

James said, still protesting his new role as caregiver. Until Meghan, the clan had lived peacefully for the most part.

"We have been lucky in that regard, but my word is final. You will do your best by her and, by the gods, she will survive this or die swiftly before suffering too much pain. I trust in you, James. You will do right by this woman."

James looked out over the ocean. Almost every fiber of his being wanted to give chase. But chances were Meghan would be pulling up to the Rhode Island coastline soon. "Can you at least see if anyone is available to track Meghan? She should be docking close to Point Judith. Make sure they know not to fight her, just track her until Ian and Roark can join me in the hunt. I will not have any of our people killed trying to stop her. I can't stress enough how powerful she's become. As for the mortals, we can only hope that our chase will keep her from harming any of them."

"Consider it done."

James took a deep breath then another. Very quietly, he said, "I'm sorry I've failed you."

"You haven't failed. You have done well, my son, and you make us all proud. No other could have found the rogue wolf as fast as you have. It is only a matter of time before Meghan is captured." The king said goodbye after securing a promise that James would keep him updated on the young one's progress.

Closing his cell phone, James placed his hand on the wooden rail and looked out at the bright moon. It was late night, perhaps even early morning and he wanted nothing more than to shift and run free along the cool sands of the beach. He couldn't, not here, not where he might be detected. Plus, he couldn't leave the changing mortal in his care. The next several weeks were going to be a living hell for her and if she survived, he'd have to tell her the truth of what she'd become.

5

Claudia moved in and out of consciousness, fighting the darkness to become aware of her surroundings, only to fight awareness to escape the pain. Terrifying dreams that made no real sense haunted her, until everything she saw was a jumble of time and place. It was as if a voice in her head told her a story, a long history that made no sense.

Whenever she did manage to open her eyes, she'd see *him*, the man from the shower. Vague memories tickled her thoughts but they were so unreal she couldn't believe that she'd actually had unprotected sex with a complete stranger. So the incident became another thought entwined within her dreams.

Most of the time, the man would be pacing, like a

wild tiger captured and caged in the zoo, endlessly trying to get past the invisible bars that held him from her. But if he was so restless, why didn't he just leave her? Her room changed and once she even thought she was on the water, rocking back and forth in tireless rhythm. She knew there was something wrong with her. But why was she here and not in a hospital? The fleeting questions left her as quickly as they came. Nothing made sense.

Pain turned from white-hot fever to bitter cold in an instant, only to switch back again. The man took care of her. Sometimes she heard his voice, a low growling sound that said things she didn't really comprehend. All she knew was there was comfort in the tone of his words, safety in the presence of his administering hands. Occasionally his face was present in the history of her dream world—standing apart from the crowd, watching from the edge of firelight, whether on a sandy beach or in a castle hall.

"Where are we?" Claudia croaked, seeing her caretaker for once sitting in a chair near a table. This was the first time she felt well enough to speak to him, even though she'd tried before. A book lay across his lap but he paid more attention to the night skyline out the window than the pages before him.

Seeing him was surreal. How was it that she was being taken care of by such a handsome man?

The four-poster bed featured light wood carved into columns. Stiff material, heavily printed with pastel floral design, decorated the curtains and bed. Whatever this place was, it looked more like some old woman's house or bed-and-breakfast than a hotel. Behind the man, she saw a hint of a white kitchen, though the room was shadowed in darkness.

"You're awake," he said, like it was a great revelation. Standing, he set the book aside and walked over to the bed. "I wasn't sure you would wake up again. You've been very ill."

"Why am I not in a hospital?" She turned her head to watch him. Her neck was stiff but the blinding white heat was gone. "I should see a doctor."

"They can't help you with this. They wouldn't know what to do for you and would only end up making things worse."

"And you can help me?" She tried to sit but the effort was weak. In the end, he had to help her up. Strong hands wrapped around her upper arms, lifting her with ease. The warmth of his palms sent a shiver over her, causing her to become very aware of how close he was. For some reason, she imagined she remembered what his lips felt like on hers. But that was impossible, for she would definitely remember kissing a man like him and her body wasn't sore, as it surely would have been if she'd fucked him like she'd dreamt she had.

"I hope I can." He let go and she felt an acute disappointment at his withdrawal. "What is your name?"

"Claudia Hughes. And you?"

"James O'Connell."

"A name to go with the face." She smiled slightly. It was a simple enough discovery but now she could stop thinking of him as the handsome caretaker. "Are we still on the island? I thought I felt water, or was I dreaming?"

"No, we're in Connecticut, near the New York state line."

"What?" she exclaimed. That surprised her. "What are we doing in Connecticut? I'm supposed to be in Rhode Island. I have a room, my camera and my suitcase and my car..." She took a deep breath, mentally checking her limbs. Years of training in the gym had left her strong and able to protect herself if needed, not that she felt threatened by James.

"I'm sorry. There was no time to stay. I'll make a call and have someone pick your things up for you and keep them safe." He looked as if he would say more but instead he stood up.

"What are you? Some kind of secret agent? FBI? ATF? CDC? FDA? Who?" She gave a nervous laugh. "A psycho killer?"

"Would a killer keep you alive for over two weeks?" he asked, arching an amused brow.

"Ah." She gave another nervous laugh. She'd been asleep for two weeks? By the stiff ache in her body, she had little doubt he was telling the truth. Besides, there was something in his eyes that begged to be both trusted and obeyed. "No, probably not."

"All you need to know right now is you're very sick. The fact that you're awake is a good sign but the pain is not over. I'm the only one who can help you right now and you're going to have to trust me on that." His expectant look prodded her to nod.

"Okay," she agreed. "But I only say that because I'm too weak to run away from you. I doubt I could even make it to the bathroom on my—" Claudia felt the blood draining from her face. "Oh Gawd."

"What is it? Is the pain worsening?"

"Two weeks? Um, you've taken care of my..." Mortified, she glanced around the room, finally settling on the bathroom door. She couldn't think of anything worse than this incredibly handsome man tending to her "private needs". "I am so sorry."

He gave a small laugh, the first she could recall really hearing from him. "Don't worry about it. Your condition made such concerns a moot point. The only thing I did was get you into a shower and into some of my clothes."

At that, Claudia glanced down, blushing. She did indeed wear an oversized t-shirt and pants that were rolled at the waist. Then the thought that he'd held her naked when she was completely unaware made her blush deepen. He wasn't talking like an intimate lover so she decided she wouldn't either. His tone only confirmed that she had hallucinated about the sex in the shower.

But even so, had he touched her as he dressed her? Did he think she was pretty? Was he in the shower with her when he bathed her? Naked and wet, his muscled body would be a perfectly delicious temptation to any woman. And why was her mind always returning to the passionate parts of her dreams when there was so much more happening to her right now?

Her heartbeat sped up in her chest, thumping harder than she ever remembered it beating. Suddenly James frowned in concentration. Grabbing her face, he turned her to look at him. His eyes pierced into hers, as if examining them.

"This isn't right, it's too soon," he said to himself. Then addressing her, he asked, "Does your skin prickle?"

"No." She tried to shake her head in denial but he held it steady.

"Open your mouth. Let me see your teeth."

Claudia obeyed the strange command, parting her lips slightly. He reached inside with a finger, poking around at her gums and teeth. She made a weak noise, jerking back. "Hey, I'm not some thoroughbred horse you're checking out."

For a moment, he looked confused before suddenly laughing, a sound deep and richer than before. When he'd finished, he asked, "Can you eat?"

Claudia nodded, not realizing how hungry she was until he asked.

"Good, I'll be right back. Do not leave this room."

Claudia nodded again, though really, where would she go? When he'd left, she forced her body to slowly move. First, she checked the guest folder left by the telephone. It did indeed say she was at the Margotte Bed-and-Breakfast in Greenwich, Connecticut. She didn't even remember being in a car, let alone traveling across two states.

She threw a few punches in the air, trying to work the kinks out of her muscles. Weightlifting and kickboxing made for great workouts, even if she didn't really use her skills for fighting. Fear of what was going to happen tried to work its way through her but she pushed it back, not wanting to give in to weakness. Besides, something inside her, a deep whisper, said she was safe with James and that everything was going to be all right. Her mother had taught her to listen to that voice, no matter how quiet hers seemed to be in comparison to the other women in her family.

Catching her reflection in the mirror over the dresser, she flinched. The horrific creature looking back at her could not be her! She stumbled toward the mirror, touching her face in dismay. Dark circles marred her eyes and her hair was a jumbled mess of curls. What little tan she normally had was completely washed out of her complexion. "I look like death warmed over."

Pulling up her hair, she turned to see her neck. A large bruise centered around a half-dozen, perfectly formed, puncture marks right above her artery. Lightly, she pressed against the skin, only to flinch as a twinge of pain worked its way across her throat. What kind of animal had attacked her? A dog?

Claudia couldn't remember a dog. In fact, she couldn't remember much beyond eating her salad all alone at the Block Island restaurant. Dropping her hair, she instantly walked toward the bathroom. If she was going to be traveling with Mr. Handsome, she'd need to look a little more presentable—if only to make herself feel better.

Taking a fast shower, she used the shampoo provided by the bed-and-breakfast and the razor James had left by the sink. It wasn't a vast improvement but at least the heat from the shower put a flush to her cheeks that had been missing before. Afterward, she borrowed his brush. Silky, dark strands wove through the bristles, the exact color of James' hair. Without her own clothes, she put James' t-shirt and exercise pants back on, pulling the drawstring and rolling them at the waist. The idea that he'd bathed and changed her made her blush.

Glancing out the window at the small parking area lit by a single light, she searched for James. It was late, nearly twelve o'clock by what the alarm clock said. Not seeing him, she moved to sit on the bed, turning on the television as she waited for the food.

"YOU SHOULD FEEL like getting up after you've had some protein," James said as he opened the door. He carried two plastic sacks in one hand and a drink tray in the other. Kicking the door shut, he looked at Claudia in surprise. The fresh scent of soap enhanced her natural smell. Water had soaked into her shirt along her shoulders where the hair touched and her dark locks clung to her neck, hiding the bruise beneath the wet tresses. The soft light from the television screen illuminated her in a flickering glow, casting her features almost blue. The low tones of whatever movie she watched filled the room. He had detected the voices before he stepped inside and knew it to be some romantic comedy by the way the actresses spoke.

Claudia still wore no bra, because after he'd showered her, he hadn't bothered to put the one she owned back on her. He saw no point in it as she slept all the time anyway, writhing in pain. The lacy undergarment was tucked safely away in his suitcase. He swallowed hard, his body stirring to attention. It wasn't an amazing feat. The last weeks had been hell as he carried and cared for her. Knowing she was right there, so close, so touchable, had been torment and no amount of self-stimulated release was going to cure him of the affliction of lust that now made a constant course through his veins.

Moving to put the sacks on the table, he knew what the next part of her changing might bring—though so far she'd proven herself quite different than the others—if her little performance in the shower the first night was any indication. After she fed, she'd have more strength but she'd also have the heady power of the lycans inside her. In what form that power decided to first show itself remained to be seen. One man he'd helped tried to rip his head off—not that he'd gotten very far for his great effort. Turned lycans were no match for a natural-born—at least not at first. The poor guy almost made the full transformation but died during his first shift. From what their doctors said, his heart just exploded in his chest.

A pang of fear washed over him as he thought of Claudia's heart exploding. Of course there was no way to tell what would happen to her, no way to stop it if it did. All he could do was wait and try to keep her safe—from both the outside world and herself. Traveling with her, he'd had plenty of time to study and worry over her. She was so delicate, so small compared to some of the men he'd helped through the changing—even some of the women for that matter. It was hard to believe she'd stood up to Meghan, even when he'd heard her fighting for himself.

Already he'd told his father that he didn't know how well her body would hold up. The king had been sorry to hear the news but merely ordered him to do his best by her. With Meghan being one of them, they all felt responsible for the rogue lycan's deeds. All the deaths she caused were on their hands as surely as if they'd killed the people themselves.

Ian had been tracked down in Calcutta, India, with Ceana a couple of days ago. They were on their way back to join him, though James suggested maybe Ceana would be more comfortable staying with one of the other clan members until the threat of Meghan had passed. Ian was a patient leader and immensely loyal. He took great pride in his history, family and traditions. He guarded those things with his life and would be a fierce companion when it came to hunting down a threat to their clan.

Roark had not been heard from, though it was hardly surprising. Since his wife, Natasha, belonged to the *Farfadet* race, a supernatural people known to live in frozen points of time rather than an actual place, she tended to not pay attention to the cycle of days like other races did. Funny, since all other points of ladylike etiquette were drilled into her head. And Roark's easygoing nature didn't exactly make him punctual.

"I see you were able to take a shower," he said to break the silence. She hadn't answered him when he walked in.

"Oh yeah. I hope you don't mind. I used your brush." Claudia made a weak noise and he turned to study her.

"Why would I mind?" He arched a brow.

"I'm starved. Is that steak I smell?" She pushed up from the bed, not acknowledging his somewhat rhetorical question. He kept his senses on alert as he began removing the takeout food containers from the bags. "It smells really good."

The breathiness of her words as she came to stand next to him made his gut tighten. She braced her hands on the back of the chair, sniffing as she leaned forward. The position wasn't meant to be seductive but seeing her bent over, knowing she'd be naked beneath the oversized pants, set his libido on fire.

His hand trembled and he found himself reaching to touch her ass, remembering every detail of what it looked like from the torturous time he'd bathed her. Then he'd kept his hands to himself but, now that she was awake, he wanted nothing more than to strip her down once more. Drawing his fingers back before he made contact with her body, he reached for a plastic fork and handed it to her.

"It's just steak?" Claudia scrunched up her brow. "They didn't have any side dishes to go with it?"

James gave a small smile. The waitress at the local diner had looked at him like he was crazy when he placed his order, but he'd learned from past mistakes that a diet of all meat helped the process along. "Trust me, the sides are just fillers. You'll want the meat."

"But rare?" She wrinkled her nose.

He didn't answer as he took a switchblade from his pocket and flicked it open. The serrated edge was clean and would have to do for a cutting utensil. When he handed it over to her, he saw an amber glint flickering inside her eyes. It was the primal stirring of the beast growing within her. "Eat. It'll help you feel better."

6

CLAUDIA WASN'T sure how she managed but she mindlessly devoured three T-bones and part of a tenderloin steak. Rare meat wasn't normally her first choice but there was something to the flavor. It was almost orgasmic and each bite caused a small shiver of pleasure to work over her limbs.

She felt strong, powerful. Her heart beat heavy and fast, like she could do anything. The wound on her neck tingled and the dim light in the room didn't seem as dark as before. Her eyes must have adjusted, because she could now see into the shadows with ease.

"What was in that food?" she asked, breathing hard as she pushed up from the table. "I feel funny."

The tingling in her neck worked its way down

her spine, spreading throughout her limbs. Her skin erupted with heat, a fire that blazed up from her core. Then a smell invaded her senses, the subtle scent of shampoo and musk. The fire turned to passion, causing a deep ache inside her pussy. Her nipples tightened and she became aware of how little of a barrier the t-shirt provided.

James sat at the end of the bed. He hadn't eaten with her, merely watched, making small talk about the warm weather and that a weatherman predicted rain. She had the impression he wanted to say more, much more, but held back, keeping to the mundane and unimportant.

As she walked toward him, mindless as to her intent, he stiffened. "Try to breathe, Claudia. I don't want to have to hurt you but, if you attack me, I will be forced to restrain you."

A deep shudder moved along her arms and she balled her hands into fists. Her breathing became heavier and she couldn't control it. Something inside her was changing. Passion and violence filled her thoughts until she wasn't sure if she wanted to hit James or kiss him.

"Something's wrong with..." She tried to hold on to her reasoning, tried to stop the images of blood and sex from entering her mind. She saw James in the shower, his thick cock fisted in his hand, remembered the sound of his passionate grunts as he brought himself to release. The image of bloody fangs interrupted the sexual thoughts and she recalled a woman's face contorting into that of a wolf. The dreams she'd had over the last two weeks surfaced, trying to form a complete picture in her mind, a series of events that would equal an immortal life. She remembered fur sprouting, fangs and claws growing into sharp points. A werewolf? She didn't even believe in such things. It must have been some movie she'd watched, book she'd read...or was it real?

Claudia reached for her neck. The memory *was* real. White-hot pain had seized her as the woman bit into her neck. But how was such a thing possible? A she-wolf?

Confused, she lifted her hands, ready to lash out. Rage poured from inside her and she went for the closest target. Never had she felt so angry. As she lunged forward, her hands met flesh. James grunted, his eyes wide as she clawed at his shirt. He fell back on the bed and lifted his knee, pressing it into her stomach. She flipped over his head, landing on her back. Her feet struck the headboard hard, sending a reverberating shock through her system.

James spun around as if to crawl over her head.

She pushed off the headboard, flinging her body to the side so she rolled off the bed. Power filled her but she didn't know how to control it. James stood, his movements perfect and stealthy. Claudia called up all her training, though a kickboxing workout wasn't exactly the same thing as hand-to-hand combat. Still, she swung, putting a practiced force behind her punch.

He caught her fists in rapid succession and a strange glow came to his eyes. "Easy, young one. You're like a little kitten trapped in a corner. You cannot hurt me and you'll only hurt yourself if you try. I have no wish to bind you, but I will if you force my hand."

Claudia tried to hit him again, jerking her arms to free her hands, not understanding why her body was acting the way it was. She wasn't a violent person and yet she needed to strike out. His grip tightened, keeping her from pulling her fist away. Her mouth opened wide and she let loose a short, breathy growl.

James laughed. "You're a fierce one, aren't you, little tigress? So brave in the face of danger."

She tried to jerk her hand free. When she couldn't, she kicked, sweeping her leg around, hoping he would be forced to let go of her fist. Her calf met the steel of solid flesh and James laughed, unmoved by her strike. Her gaze fell to his mouth, the slight curve when he smiled drawing her notice. The brown waves of his hair framed his firm lips and strong jaw. The images of blood left, replaced with the thought of him in the shower, stroking himself to completion.

Without thought, she lifted up on her toes and leaned her face to his, lightly nipping at that sexy smile. His height made it hard to reach him but the angle of his face toward hers allowed her to bite at his bottom lip, pulling it slightly with her teeth before letting go. Though the nip had been soft, when she looked again, she saw a small dot of blood beaded where she'd bitten him. Claudia leaned forward once more, pressing her mouth gently to his. She slipped her tongue over the rim, strangely drawn to taste the tiny wound she'd made.

A low groan filled her as James responded. His hold on her fist lessened and she slipped her hands away, striking him on the shoulder several times without breaking their kiss, before grabbing hold of his t-shirt to hold him close. His mouth roughly ground against hers, each pass of his lips harder than before. Claudia moaned. James' hands found her hips and he worked his fingers into her pants, pushing the loose material down. It fell away from her body and Claudia kicked it away with her feet.

He pulled his mouth from hers, his piercing brown eyes locking onto her gaze as he slowly sat down before her on the bed. Warm palms ran down her legs, touching her knees only to come back up. Her skin felt extra-sensitive since she'd shaved and each movement reverberated throughout her entire system. James reached around, squeezing her ass, kneading the cheeks so they spread considerably.

"Ah," she gasped as an intense shock wave of pleasure shot through her. Wet, hot cream flooded her pussy. James' eyes narrowed and he inhaled deeply through his nose. A primordial need tightened his features and he gripped her ass harder, dragging her hips forward until her stomach pressed against his face.

The soft glow from the television flashed over his skin, contrasting with his chiseled features. His hands worked the oversized t-shirt up, revealing her stomach. James kissed her hipbone, running light caresses over her flat stomach to her navel. Gently, he drew his tongue around her belly button. Claudia slipped her fingers into his hair, wanting more.

He continued to explore, touching her back and waist, sliding his hands around to cup her breasts.

Pinching her nipples, he made a loud, animalistic noise of pleasure. Everything about him was primal and raw, from the way he moved to the way he boldly touched her.

His kisses became more aggressive, moving lower over her hips until they reached the short thatch of hair growing between her thighs. Claudia pulled at his shirt, wanting to feel the heat of his naked flesh against hers. He took his hands from her breasts, letting her undress him. Throwing the t-shirt aside, she pushed at his shoulders, knocking him back on the bed.

"Thank you for saving me from that woman," she said, lowering her jaw. "I remember her now. She haunted my dreams and I doubted it was real."

"Meghan is very real," he assured her. "And very evil. She tried to kill you."

"I don't want to talk about her right now," Claudia whispered, stroking back his chin-length hair. "I only wished to thank you and to tell you that I'd like to properly show you my appreciation for what you did."

❈

"Don't fight the memories. They can help you." James ignored the disgust he felt at the selfish comment. Sure, they could help her understand what was happening, but the sooner she accepted her connection to Meghan, the sooner he could use her to hunt the rogue killer. "Tell me what happened. What do you remember?"

"I remember now how she came for me, bit me, how she changed," Claudia whispered as clarity filtered through her gaze. The instant was brief and when she stared back at him, she was again looking as if she wanted to devour him, like she had looked at the steak before tearing into it. The protein had made her stronger, hopefully strong enough to save her life, but it also kicked her primal instincts into overdrive. Luckily for him, it was now sex she craved and not blood. He hadn't been sure when she had begun to hit him.

He pushed up on his elbows as she pulled at her shirt. The material lifted, revealing her smooth, perfect thighs. He held his breath, watching intently as the curtain rose over her pussy. Next came her stomach and breasts, small, perfect mounds with taut nipples begging to be sucked. His cock hardened even more, pressing against his pants.

Without waiting, she lunged forward, her lengthened nails biting into his chest as she straddled his legs. Claudia scratched a painful trail over his muscles, causing a thin line of blood to follow her movements. She reached his pants, pulling the denim material so hard the button slipped from the loop and the zipper ripped apart. Her palm found the silk of his boxers, rubbing his thick cock through the opening she'd made.

"I don't know what's gotten into me but I can't seem to stop and think," she admitted, stroking him frantically. "All I want is to get you into bed."

"Argh," he groaned, automatically reaching out to pull her down to him. His mouth met a soft breast and he sucked it deep, his lips moving crazily along the supple skin. All thoughts of tracking Meghan slipped from his mind.

Claudia pulled at his waistband, as if trying to rid him of his jeans. When she didn't succeed, she slipped her breast from his mouth and sat up, grinding her pussy against his cock. The silk boxers instantly moistened, covering his shaft with the wet heat of her sex.

Her head rolled back and she gave a pretty sigh. The firm mattress molded to his back as her slender form tried to keep him pinned down. Her legs clamped around his hips and her body tightened. He again felt his mind trying to connect with her, trying to build a mind-link so they could share thoughts, so he could know her fully. Like before, in the shower, he resisted the connection, not wanting to build one without her consent. No matter how much he wanted to know everything about her, he would not force the information from her any more than he had to.

James took hold of her arms and flipped her onto her back, pushing her up on the bed by her thighs as he walked his knees forward. Primitive noises escaped him as he frantically worked the jeans from his hips. Every subtle brush against his cock drove him mad with lust. By the time he freed his penis from the silken prison of the boxers, he was ready to explode. The last two weeks taking care of her had been torment and now that she was beneath him, so warm and naked, her pussy wet and sweet, he couldn't force himself to slow down.

He pressed his thick cock tightly against her moist slit and wet himself in her cream. She trembled violently with each stroke, making weak noises of pleasure and encouragement.

"You're so big," she panted, pressing her hips to meet his. She closed her eyes tight. "Mmm, yeah, feels so good, just like that."

James grunted his response, forcing the beast from his eyes and body. He didn't want her to see it in him, not now, not when it could scare her away and make her stop touching him. His body throbbed, aching to thrust into the sweet, tight hold of her cunt.

"Tell me you want this," he commanded.

"Yes," she gasped.

"I don't want to hurt you but I also want to fuck you so hard."

Suddenly her eyes opened wide. The supernatural yellow in her gaze blocked out all brown. A low growl sounded in the back of her throat. She threw her legs around his waist, grabbing tight as she tried to force him inside her hot pussy.

Her mouth opened with a harsh breath, showing the delicate points of emerging fangs. A primal grumble entered her voice as she said, "Say it again."

"I don't want to hurt you." He grunted as she rocked her hips away from him, only to thrust up again. He kept his stroke gentle and easy.

"Not that, the other."

James grinned a little. "I want to fuck you hard."

"Mmm," she moaned, rolling her head as if the very words turned her on. "Say it again."

"I'm going to fuck you hard." James punctuated the words with an experimental jab forward into her soft pussy, not rough, but no longer as tender as before. She moaned louder, her eyes rolling back in her head. "You want it? Huh? You want me to fuck you?"

She moaned again, nodding frantically. Her legs fell to the side, parting wide, offering her sexy body to him. Her features flushed with a healthy glow, her skin darkening more than before. He pulled back, again giving an experimental thrust to test how she reacted to the slightly rougher handling.

"Yes," she breathed, belatedly answering his question.

"Yes, what?"

At that she paused. "Yes, sir?"

James hid his smile, finding he liked the almost-submissive way she commanded him. With those few, hesitant words, she had given him permission to dominate. The lycan inside him howled with pleasure, begging to be freed, begging to mark this rare find of a woman as its own so no other lycan would dare to touch her without his express permission. The possessive feelings were a new experience for him and he pushed them aside, not wishing to delve too deeply into the thoughts.

James knew he couldn't control the beast forever, so instead he ordered her to turn around. She obeyed, flipping onto her stomach. Her pert ass beckoned and he spread her legs from behind, slipping his cock between her pussy and the mattress.

"Mmm," she moaned, continuing the soft pleas, now muffled by the mattress. She trembled and he felt her cream warming his cock as he slowly moved against her.

"Ah, that's it. Get me wet just like in the shower. I need your slick juices lubricating me so I can fuck this sexy ass of yours."

For the first time since she'd started, Claudia appeared to hesitate. "What?"

James couldn't help the slightly dominant surge that filtered through him at her innocent question. "Mmm, yeah, I'm going to hold you down and stick my cock in this sweet ass of yours. I've wanted to fuck it ever since I saw it naked. I'm going to break you open and ride you so good, sweetheart."

She tried to push up but he pressed a hand to her upper back, purposefully forcing her breasts against the bed. He maneuvered his body so that his cock sank into the tight fit of her sex, wetting in her cream. Then, withdrawing, he drew it up to her ass. The bend of his knees forced her legs to stay open as he drew the mushroomed tip along the cleft, spreading her cheeks, torturing her with the slow, purposeful movements.

She began to shake and her body tightened as he pressed close to the rosette. He grunted as her cheeks gripped the head of his cock. In one single movement, he had her hips angled up toward him and positioned to take him in. With his hands on each side of her hips, he spread her cheeks farther and pressed his shaft between them to probe her opening.

"James, I'm not sure this is a good idea—*oh!*" The last word came out as a moan.

Encouraged, he slipped the tip into her ass, practically howling at the intense pleasure.

"James, you're too big—*ah!*" Her voice had become a low whisper.

He moved deeper still, stretching her ass to his size by rocking back and forth. The look of her swallowing him up was almost too erotic to bear. He pushed harder, driven by primal need.

"That's right. You like it, don't you, *a thaisce?*" he whispered, trying to relax her.

"Ah." It wasn't a shouted yes, but it also wasn't a firm no. Heartened by her response, he pressed forward. He closed his eyes in rapture. Most women he'd been with tried to take control, turned sex into a power struggle. Claudia was different. She let him take command.

"Spread your legs, relax for me. I only want to make you feel so good." James grinned. She opened her legs like he told her to and the action caused her muscles to relax around him. This time he seated himself fully to the hilt, his aching balls pressing against the softer cheeks of her ass. "Ah, there it is. You feel so good. Your sweet ass is accepting me. I am going to fuck you so hard."

She gave a light moan. He pulled out slightly, keeping his movements slow and shallow. When he felt her trust back at him—little, hesitant thrusts to take him in—he began to move faster and harder.

"Get on your hands." He pushed her legs forward so she was on all fours. The position gave him better leverage and he grabbed hold of her hips. He thrust in full and forcefully. She gasped and he did it again. "Tell me to ride you hard."

"Ah," she panted.

"I said tell me to ride you hard." He thrust again, wanting to hear her seductive voice.

"Yes," she panted, "ride me."

James grabbed her hair, pulling it as he fucked her. He leaned forward slightly, watching the side of her breast bob with each movement. A light sheen of sweat glistened over her flesh. He pumped his hips, reveling in the tight fit as he completely broke open her virgin ass. Commanding her, he ordered, "Tell me to fuck you."

"Yes," she pleaded. "Yes."

Vaguely, he noticed she didn't actually say the word *fuck* but seemed to get hotter when he did. The fleeting thought that he'd have to make her talk dirty to him later filtered through his mind. The idea of her soft, sweet voice forming naughty little words, perhaps begging to suck his cock and drink his cum, made him jerk violently.

James couldn't think. Claudia's hands clawed at the bed linen, haphazardly scratching the material in loud rips.

"Pinch your nipples for me," he ordered.

She did, grabbing her breasts and rubbing them hard. Almost instantly, her body began to tighten and he almost screamed with relief. He wasn't sure he could hold back much longer. Her entire body stiffened as she came. James met his release seconds after, his body jerking hard. His loud, raspy groan filled the room, punctuated by her harsh breathing.

Claudia fell limp onto the mattress and he pulled away from her. When James looked at her face, he saw she slept. He wished he could take credit for screwing her to the point of exhaustion but he knew it was her condition. As her body changed, it would go through bouts of tiredness and energy, taking her on an emotional roller-coaster ride. He knelt beside her, reaching for her turned face. When he lifted her upper lip, the fangs were retracted back into her gums.

"Half of the way there," he whispered to her, suddenly desperate to have her survive it. The possessive feelings came back, bursting forth in him. Strange that they would hit him in the aftermath as well. Not resisting what he felt, he lay beside her, pulling her into his arms. Lightly kissing her temple, he whispered, "Two more weeks until your first full moon, the final test."

7

"You're sure it's Meghan?" James asked, gripping his cell phone tight.

"Randall's been out of the game for a century or so, but he's a solid tracker," Roark answered. "I don't know him too well but our father says he's good. Randall says she's heading south through New Jersey toward Atlantic City. Natasha and I just got back from her father's castle but I'm on the first flight out of Kansas City. I'll meet you in Atlantic City, hopefully getting there before she does. I'll scout all the obvious places. We still have a few contacts there who owe me favors. I should be able to find out what hotel she's registered at, even with their privacy policies well in place."

"Damn it! I'm just on my way north through

New York state like Randall said. She must have gone north and then doubled back to throw me off. Though Atlantic City does make more sense. She always was the gambler." James cursed, glancing to the bed. Four nights had passed and Claudia hadn't awakened. That didn't stop him from hauling her all over Connecticut and New York as he tried to track Meghan. The woman proved to be ever elusive and with Claudia in tow, unconscious, he couldn't get too close to his target. However, he did stay on her trail. Catching Meghan was too important to let her slip by.

"Natasha isn't coming with you?" James forced his eyes from Claudia's unmoving form. Her strength amazed him. In the face of death, she'd shown more fight than anyone he'd ever met. "I thought she might be able to help me with—"

"She's pregnant," Roark said.

"What?" James genuinely smiled for the first time in days. "Congratulations, brother, that's great news."

"That's why we were late. She told me while we were away and the celebrating got out of hand." Roark chuckled. "Some of those *Farfadet* can drink."

"They freeze time," James said wryly. "They probably freeze their metabolisms too."

"Those sneaky motherfuck..." Roark let loose a long string of curses. "I thought it was strange a one-hundred-pound little slip of a girl could outdrink me."

James sighed softly, truly happy for his brother. Pregnancies were very rare for their kind. They guessed nature made it that way for a reason. If all of them bred like humans but never died, the world would be overrun with lycans. The window for pregnancy was small, usually occurring right after life-mating. If couples didn't take advantage as newly-weds then they might never get the chance.

"I understand about Natasha not coming," James said. "I don't want her in harm's way. As a magical being who lived among humans for so long, I thought she might be of help in explaining the full details to Claudia. I would send Claudia away, but we may need her, and I'd ask Ceana to come, but she seems too delicate and she doesn't like being near the ocean. Though, as I consider it, I honestly think it's better to keep your and Ian's mates safe, especially if one is carrying my nephew."

"I think she's tougher than she looks," Roark argued, "but then you always did want to protect the females."

"Just ask whatever it is you're going to ask," James said.

"What's she like?" Roark laughed, not bothering to conceal his curiosity.

James wished he could send Claudia away, even if a large part of him wanted her where he could protect her. "She's strong. She fought Meghan and even broke one of the woman's ribs."

"Damn," Roark swore. "And Meghan's pretty tough even for a lycan female."

"She's classy," James continued, his vision clouding. "The way she moves. She's refined and feminine, yet strong enough to take on Meghan. When she eats, she takes these small, delicate bites, except when the hunger takes over and she attacks the steak. There's something in her eyes too, an innocence almost and intelligence. She's the type of person who really looks at the world but still manages to see the good. Her soul is pure and she—"

"You had some long talks, hadn't you?"

"Actually no," James realized all he'd revealed to his brother. "Our minds linked together for a brief moment and I saw inside her. I tried not to look, but I saw enough."

"Really? But that normally only happens when

you…" Roark began laughing harder. "James, you wolf, you! You've been stickin' it to your charge!"

"Don't talk about her like that," James hissed.

"Ah, I'm sorry, brother, don't get upset." Roark cleared his throat. "So is she pretty?"

James didn't answer and Roark made a knowing sound.

"The more I think about it," James said, changing the subject, "the more I think we don't need any of the women around for this. It is nasty business and I don't want to risk Meghan using them for leverage. She's already done too much damage."

"About Meghan, there's something you should know," Roark said. "She's killed two more. Both young women. Randall sniffed out their bodies alongside the interstate. The mortals haven't discovered them yet and Randall hid all evidence of a lycan attack but…"

"I know," James said when his brother didn't continue. "I hate it too. The families deserve to know the truth, they deserve closure, but we tried that route before. Most of the people we tried to explain things to had nervous breakdowns. Not only did they lose a loved one but they learned that supernatural beings existed, something their church and Hollywood tells them is evil. Mortals can't handle that kind of knowledge, at least most of them. Those who didn't go crazy ended up thinking they could become the next generation of werewolf hunters and only got themselves hurt for their trouble."

"I understand all that but, if someone killed a member of my family, I'd want the truth."

"We're not like mortals. We can handle the truth in this instance. They can't." James frowned. There was no right or wrong to this debate and both brothers knew it. "The best we can do by them is stop her from hurting anyone else."

"We should have been there with you, tracking her," Roark said, his tone low.

"What's done is done. No one knew she'd start killing again after I tracked her to Vegas. The right decision was made at the time and we determined I should go by myself. Alone, I managed to stay close on her trail. She would have sensed all three of us. Besides, you and Ian both had new brides. What matters is you're coming now. She's strong but her powers lie mostly in temptation and lust and in her ability to elude capture. We can resist her and together we will find her." It occurred to James that *he* should be the one hearing these words of comfort from his brother. The failure felt like his alone, since he'd been charged with taking her down.

"I'll call you when my flight lands."

"I'll see you there. Make sure you try the hotels with spas first. She's most likely to go where she can be pampered."

"Will do," Roark said. "Be safe."

"Yeah, you too." James hung up the phone. Every part of him wanted to jump in the small rental car and begin driving, but he couldn't force more road hours on Claudia, even if she did restlessly sleep through them. Her body was in a delicate state and the jostling couldn't be good for her.

"Who is Meghan?"

James swung his attention from the phone to Claudia. Her eyes were open, steadily on him as she pushed up from the bed. Days of sleep had tousled her hair around her face in a mess of unkempt curls. Despite her appearance, her wide eyes were clear. "Don't you remember? She attacked you."

"Yes, but who is she?"

"Just a very bad someone I have to find."

"Am I one of the women you are trying to protect from her?" Claudia rolled her neck, stretching her arms to the side. She seemed more interested in him than in their new surroundings.

"What do you mean?" How much of the conversation had she heard?

"Just now, you said 'The more I think about it, the more I think we don't need any of the women around for this'. Am I one of the women you don't need around?" Almost cautiously, she pulled the covers from her legs. For the first time, she took her eyes from his, glancing down over her body and noticing the female pajama pants and tighter t-shirt he'd dressed her in. "Is someone going to try to use me for leverage?"

James frowned. He'd been so careful to keep his conversations out of her earshot but tonight he'd gotten careless, not stepping outside to handle his business like he should have. "It's nothing to worry yourself over. You need to concentrate on getting better."

"I feel better," Claudia answered, not sounding appeased. "I'm not some little weakling and I'd rather work through my illness than spend my days in bed, asleep." She stood beside the bed and he suppressed a smile at her confident look. "Besides, I'm not sure what it is I'm supposed to be concentrating on getting better from. The wolf-woman's bite? Is it some sort of rabies?"

James watched her face, taking a step forward. "Do you remember what happened more clearly now? It should be coming back to you."

"I didn't remember it all at first, but then after we ate, I began seeing things, clear things. I thought it might be a strange nightmare but then I heard you on the phone. You said that mortals, which I'm assuming means humans like me, don't understand the supernatural." She bit her lip in thought, her eyes narrowing. He could practically see her mind working. "I also gather you are hunting the beast that attacked me because she's killed others."

James detected a small tremor work over her but she kept a brave face. "How is it you accept this? Do you know of the lycankind?"

"Aside from movies and books?" she chuckled. "No."

"Then how is it you accept?" He waited for the hysteria, the tears and pleas. They didn't come.

"I suppose because I always wanted there to be something like that in the world—something beyond scientific explanation—and because of my grandmother and mom. They believed in things that couldn't be seen with their eyes."

"What things? Vampires? Fairies?"

At that, she looked startled. Her mouth opened as if she wanted to ask him something but then she slowly shook her head in denial. "In the abilities of the human brain—telepathy, visions of the past and future, past-life regressions, stuff like that. They even had special gifts, psychic abilities if you want to call them that. They'd get premonitions. They used to tell me real ghost stories and my grandmother said she could communicate with the dead. Is it a far stretch to go from ghosts to other supernatural creatures?"

"And you?" James asked curiously. It had been a really long time since he'd met a psychic. There weren't too many real ones around anymore. Most of them with the potential never explored and developed the gift.

"I have feelings, nothing like they had. My grandmother used to help police officers solve murder cases. My mom always said that it was that work that drained her soul and eventually killed her. No one can see that kind of stuff without being affected. My mom died in a car wreck. Funny how she didn't see that one coming, huh?" The joke was a weak effort to hide the pain she had to feel at the memory. "They also dabbled in the craft but, by the time I was at an age I wanted to learn, they were gone."

James nodded slowly.

"And you? Are you some kind of, what did you call it, a wolf hunter?"

"Something like that." It wasn't a lie, just not the

clarification she probably wanted to hear. "What do you remember about your attack?"

"I remember eating by myself at a local restaurant on the island, looking at the ferry schedule and contemplating if I wanted to stay another few nights or go on toward Maine like I'd originally planned before getting sidetracked."

"Why were you sidetracked?" James listened intently, trying to pick up why Meghan might have chosen Claudia as a target. Did it have something to do with her heritage? Or was she just a random pick?

"You know that whole psychic thing I was telling you about? I just 'felt' I needed to go to Block Island, so I turned the car and went there. I felt kind of silly once I got there. I feel even sillier now knowing what I ended up finding."

"What happened after you checked the schedule?" James prompted.

"I walked back toward my hotel. Some woman suddenly appeared and then everything went black. By the time I came to, I was by the ocean being bitten by a woman with the features of a wolf. I tried to fight her off and actually got a few good punches in. She wasn't too pleased with my resistance and in the end was too strong for me to fight. When she bit me the first time, it was like a kiss, but the second time, it hurt like hell, the kind of searing, white-hot, burning hell a person can't even describe. Everything went dark and then I remember waking up to find you..." Claudia blushed, her face flaming, and she looked to the floor.

James remembered well the state she'd found him in—showering with his cock in hand. He also remembered the sweet way she'd fucked him that night. His cock stirred at the memory, causing a deep ache that never seemed to go away when she was awake and only tempered itself when she was passed out.

Claudia continued, "Ah, you had, ah, rescued me. I know you've been taking care of me for two weeks now and I know that last night I, ah, showed my, um, that we..." She turned her eyes to him. "Didn't we?"

"Not last night," he said, his tone lowering. The memory of it invaded his senses. His dick remembered all too well the tight fit of her pussy, the glide of her cream. His mouth tasted her nipples, felt their budded texture. And his hands ached to once again touch her soft flesh. He'd managed to keep from going to her while she was asleep, though it was hard to keep his hands to himself, but now arousal coursed through him. "Four days have passed since then."

"Four?" She glanced around the hotel room. It was nothing special, just some random roadside inn he'd found off the interstate in some small town. The dark carpet and pastel-shaded walls accented the floral pattern on the bed. A small television with crappy reception, a worn dresser, chipped mirror on the wall, a tiny bathroom with shower and a nightstand with a corded phone were the only items in the place. The night after they'd had sex, he'd gotten a nicer hotel, hoping for a repeat of the sexual events. She had slept. The second night, the place was not as grand as the first but definitely nicer than this. Again she'd slept. So the last two nights, thinking she'd be out for a week again, he'd just taken the first thing he could find. It figured that this would be the hotel room she woke up to. "Where are we now?"

"New York."

"City?"

"No, the state. I'm sorry about the room. It's the only one I could find with vacancies." Okay, so it was only a small lie. The truth was he hadn't really looked past this one hotel when he decided to stop for the night.

"And tomorrow where will we be?" Claudia tilted her head to the side. Her expression was unintentionally coy.

"New Jersey."

"To stop Meghan?"

"Yes."

"Will I be awake long enough to help?" She made a weak noise that resembled humor. "I want to help. I know self-defense and I can..." she weakly shrugged, "I can do something."

"The sleeping is normal for your condition." James found himself moving toward her, subtly getting closer as they spoke. The sweet scent of her body, the natural perfume of woman, captured his keen sense of smell. "But even if you do stay awake, I do not want you confronting her."

"And what is my condition? You never explained." She reached for her neck but the bruises she sought had healed, leaving behind perfectly smooth skin. The signs of her turning were good but he knew better than to get his hopes up.

"You were bitten by a lycan."

"And that means?" Again she tried to be brave but he detected the speeding of her heart, the shiver that worked over her spine, the small bead of sweat that formed along her hairline near the temple.

"You're sick."

"I'm becoming like her, aren't I?"

"No, not like her. She is a natural-born, for you

it's different." James wondered why he was answering her when he'd rather be kissing her. Something about her lucid expression and clear eyes begged him to be honest.

"What does that mean, James?"

"It means you might die during your first full moon, if not before." Why was he talking? He shouldn't be telling her this.

"But I feel better."

"Now you do, but nothing can predict your first shift. It has not gone well for others in the past."

"Others?" Realization filled her at his look. "You're a lycan too, aren't you? I saw your eyes glow, or was I hallucinating?"

His silence was all the answer she needed.

Claudia wrapped her arms around her. "And you? Are you a natural-born? Or are you like me? Or are you something completely different?" She began to back away, shaking her head slowly. "Will you hunt me after I turn? Is that why you keep me close? I don't want to hurt anyone. I don't want to become a killer." A single tear worked its way into her gaze and she dashed it away with the back of her hand.

"I won't harm you," he answered, almost hurt by her sudden fear. Her heart was racing faster now, pounding so loud it echoed in his eardrums.

"My instincts say that's true but they also told me to go to Block Island and look what happened." She touched her neck. "My gifts were never that strong or controlled. I could be wrong."

He frowned slightly, studying her. "Were you with someone on Block Island? Someone I should contact?"

"No. I was alone."

"Anyone I should call?" he insisted.

"No family. I have work friends but they're not expecting me back until the end of the month."

"What is it you do?" Careful not to move and scare her, he listened intently to her answers. He had wondered if she had a man in her life but her words confirmed she didn't. By the tight fit of her body on his, he'd guessed she'd been celibate for some time. The fact pleased his male vanity greatly.

"I help to find bugs and reprogram computer software and then freelance part-time for different companies. Most of the time, I can work from home and don't need to go into the office." The worry came back to her expression. "I shouldn't have told you that. The smart thing would have been to say there are a bunch of people expecting me to check in and they will send help if I don't, wouldn't it? I don't know why but I seem to want to keep telling you the truth."

"I won't harm you," he said again, lifting his hand as he stepped toward her. Her back hit the wall of the small hotel room. There was nowhere she could run from him and he was glad she couldn't. The door to the outside world was behind him. She needed to hear him out. "If I wanted you dead, I would have left you on the beach. Besides, it's a little late for all that now, isn't it? After what we shared." He reached for her face, unable to resist touching her. His body became tight at the soft contact. What was it about this woman? One thought and he was aroused. One word and he became hard. One touch and everything faded but the need to lay claim.

"What are you, James?" Her beautiful eyes stared up at him, still so innocent even after what he'd told her.

"I'm a natural-born lycan but I'm also a hunter. I capture rogue wolves like Meghan and bring them to justice. You haven't hurt anyone and, if I can help it, you won't."

"Justice? You mean death, don't you?"

James didn't want to answer, didn't want her thinking of him as some kind of dealer of death. "Are you hungry? I can get you some steaks."

Her cheeks instantly reddened and she turned her face from his hand. "I remember what happened last time you fed me meat. How about a salad? I'm more of a vegetarian anyway, not for any political reason, just personal preference."

"Correction, you used to be more of a vegetarian. I think you'll find protein more to your tastes nowadays. Your first lesson, feed the wolf what it wants and it'll be easier to control." He grinned.

"So this infection I have is a separate entity? Like multiple personalities?"

"No, it's in you, part of you, it is you, but it's easier to understand if you separate the human tendencies from the wolf. You become two parts, both equally you. The wolf is just the primal, basic instincts all beings carry, only manifested. The human part is controlled and reasoned."

"And what does this wolf hiding inside me want?" Claudia took a deep breath and held it.

"To have its two very carnal appetites appeased. First is for blood, but meat will do if you stay on a steady diet of red meat. Rare is better." He let a small grin curl the sides of his mouth. "And..."

"And?" Her breathing deepened.

His eyes focused on her breasts, lifting beneath the tight shirt. Lust filled him and he liked the fact he'd put no bra on her. "Sex. There is power in blood and in orgasm. We lycans feed off both." He licked his lips, feeling very much the stalking beast as he lifted his hand to rest near her head, trapping her to the wall. Keeping his words a low, throaty growl, he said, "It is what keeps us strong, powerful, alive."

"About what happened between us..." Her soft voice and downcast eyes caused his heart to nearly stop. Did she regret she'd slept with him? "I'm glad it happened." His heart thumped hard as he studied her in surprise. Her wide brown eyes lifted to meet his and she gave a small smile.

James tried to gracefully hide his amazement at the admission, but pleasure unfurled inside him that had nothing to do with lust. Possessiveness overcame him, territorial feelings urging him to lay his scent on the woman so she would belong to him. If she survived the changing, no other lycan would dare touch her without his express permission. She would be his and his alone.

But was that fair? To lay claim to her when she didn't consent, didn't realize what it meant to be claimed by him? Sanity and reason argued with desire and instinct. Was she attracted to the golden danger in his gaze? Grateful to him for saving her life? But then again, she had said she was glad it had happened. Uncertainty was a new emotion for him, so he went with the one he did understand. Passion.

❖

"TELL ME ABOUT THE BEAST PART," Claudia said, liking the sound of his voice and wanting to learn about what was happening to her at the same time. She felt the changes inside her—strange changes that made her feel euphoric like she could fly over the entire world and never come to harm. At the same time, there was an underlying ache inside her bones and joints. She stretched her fingers carefully, feeling as if they would pop out of place at any second. "What will happen? Fangs? Fur? Will I know it's happening? Or will I just wake up with a bloody mouth and a fat belly?"

"You have watched too many horror movies on television," he said, not looking all that amused by her imagery.

"And yet I have nothing else to go on, do I? So what will happen?" Claudia wondered if she shouldn't show more fear. The truth was, she felt it, but she pushed it down, not wanting to appear weak in front of James. It was silly, to be sure, but she didn't want him to think she was a coward or couldn't handle the truth.

"Fangs, fur, yes. You'll remember turning, even if you won't be able to control it. From what I understand of those who are not born naturally but are turned from human to lycan, it's like watching yourself from inside your head—at least at first. After some time and with practice, your consciousness will take a more active role within the beast, merging together." He leaned closer, the heat of his skin radiating against her flesh.

"When?"

"The full moon." James lightly stroked her cheek with his, the stubble on his jaw scratching her skin. "If you..." he paused, restarting his words, "you will change every twenty-nine to thirty nights when the lunar cycle repeats itself. It is called the synodic period."

"Synodic?" She closed her eyes, sure he'd kiss her soon.

"From the Greek word that means coming together, referring to the sun and moon's positions with respect to each other as they shift together in the heavens." Lips brushed along hers with each word but didn't press.

"You know a lot about the moon." She pursed her mouth slightly, hoping to entice him to kiss her.

"I should. It's been a big part of my life for," again he paused, leaning back as if weighing his words, "many, many years." A small amber glint lit up in his eyes.

"Because you're controlled by the moon?"

"I was born as I am, influenced by the moon, not controlled by it. You will not be so lucky. You will change whether you wish it or not."

Claudia swallowed nervously, nodding her head to signify she understood. Everything he said seemed so bizarre, yet when he was near her like this, she didn't worry. "I don't want to hurt anyone. I couldn't live with that."

"I won't let you. I found you and I will take care of you. That I promise." James stroked her cheek, his lips finally finding hers as he kissed her. The tip of his tongue drew across the seam of her lips, probing as it passed back and forth. She opened herself to him, moaning as his tongue slipped inside her mouth. Pleasure flooded her, shooting sensitive waves of desire throughout her body. Tingling erupted along her nipples, making them hard, erect points that reached for him.

The slick folds of her pussy ached to be filled by

him until she could think of nothing else. Claudia ran her fingertips up his arms, gliding them beneath his t-shirt sleeves. James broke the kiss. Gripping him tight, she pressed her hips forward, only to dig her shoulder blades into the hard wall. A small burning sensation filled her eyes and when it stopped, the shadows covering his face didn't seem so deep. Details sprung to life—the texture of his skin, the sharp cut of his stubble, the shifting color in his eyes.

"I've had many thoughts while alone with you but I feel as if I haven't said anything I've meant to say to you." His soft, whispering breath hit her in a gentle caress. "Or those things I should say before such a moment."

"Like?"

"I think you're beautiful." The honesty in his gaze took her by surprise. He continued, "I'm sorry I was too late to save your mortal life. I selfishly am glad you're here with me, even though a great part of me wants to send you away to keep you safe."

Claudia was taken aback by the frank admission. Most men she'd dated tried to be mysterious and would never outright admit to liking a woman without being goaded. "I don't think I would feel safe if you sent me away. When I sleep, I like knowing you're there taking care of me. It's almost like I can feel your presence and you make the dreams easier to bear."

Where did that streak of candor come from? Whatever it was that made her feel safe was also making her want to trust him implicitly. Her grandmother would have said to listen to the emotion. James smiled, a true smile that reached his dark eyes. Her stomach tightened at the sight.

"I want you to..." The unfamiliar "dirty" talk wouldn't come naturally to her lips, even though it was what she felt. The vague memory that she'd ordered him to fuck her before tried to surface but instead of "Fuck me until I can't walk", she said, "Make love to me again."

"Take off your clothes." James stepped back. Pulling at his own shirt, he threw it aside and unbuttoned his pants before sitting on the bed.

Her heart thumped loudly. The glow in his gaze had not lessened. If anything, it seemed to burn brighter when she reached for her shirt. Tossing it to the floor, she slid her pants from her hips. The loose material pooled soundlessly around her ankles. James kicked off his shoes and socks, taking in every curve of her naked body. Somehow she wasn't embarrassed, not when he looked at her like that, like a starved man about to devour his favorite meal.

She stepped toward him, kneeling before reaching the bed. The stiff carpet pressed into her knees, uncomfortable but easily ignored. She ran her hands along his thighs. "Take these off."

James stood, obeying, as he pushed the unbuttoned pants from his hips. She grabbed the sides, helping the stiff denim off his legs. When she looked up, the tight, defined planes of muscles caused her thighs to tighten. Each piece of tanned flesh was carved to perfection.

The thick mass of his cock stood erect, the root buried in a soft thatch of hair. She touched his thighs, scratching her nails over the taut flesh before cupping his balls in her hand. Rolling them gently, she squeezed the soft globes, eliciting an excited groan of masculine pleasure. He still stood, so his shaft protruded above her. Claudia reached up, taking his cock in hand. Her thumb traced a protruding vein, following it from the base to the ridge of the mushroomed tip.

James trembled and he sat down on the bed, falling so hard he bounced a couple of times before settling. Claudia thrust his thighs apart, moving them aside so she could reach his cock and kiss a leisured trail down the side of his shaft. Keeping the touch intentionally light, she tormented him with her teasing caresses. After making several passes, she finally took the broad tip in her mouth.

James stiffened, jerking as she sucked him to the back of her throat. She grazed her teeth along the sides, bobbing her head up and down. Still, he was too large to take fully into her mouth, so she brought her hands to his shaft. Wrapping her fingers around him, she pumped her fists in time with her mouth.

James grunted in satisfaction. His hands dove into her hair and pulled her down hard, nearly gagging her with his length. She pushed on his knees so she could breathe and held her ground when he tried to pull her down again. As she sucked and blew in turn, their passion became a struggle for control over her movements. Animalistic growls echoed over her as he came, releasing a stream of seed down her throat. She swallowed the salty essence of him, enjoying the intimacy of it.

Suddenly James took hold of her arms and lifted her up, tossing her onto the bed. Her heart fluttered as his beautiful body crawled over her. His eyes narrowed and his jaw lowered, the beast stalking its prey. She wiggled on the bed, brushing her legs against the inside of his.

He lifted a finger and she watched in amazement as a claw grew from the tip. Lowering it to her chest, he drew a haphazard line over the valley of her breasts. The dangerously sharp claw didn't hurt but she knew if he wanted to he could instantly kill her with one slash of his hand. He traced a pattern around her breasts before circling in on a nipple.

Claudia gasped, closing her eyes, nearly mindless with the euphoria of his nearness. Her body called to him, begging for more, and his fingers willingly answered. He made a small sound of pleasure and the stroke of his claw became the stroke of his hand. Heated flesh massaged her chest, sending a tiny shiver over her entire length.

Soon lips followed his hand, kissing an erect nipple before biting it gently. James licked a hot trail along her form, exploring her fully. The taste of him was still in her mouth and his potent, raw smell filled her until every sensation she had was because of him. She explored his chest, running her hands over every inch she could reach. There was something primal about the way his body moved and tensed against her fingers and mouth. Before she realized it, she was biting at his flesh. His muscles contracted beneath her lips and he groaned, speaking to her in a rough tone in a language she didn't understand. The more she bit, the louder he cried out, his head falling back on his shoulders. A knee worked its way between her thighs. She licked a hard nipple, discovering that he liked it when she showed aggression.

Claudia trembled under the fire of his predatory gaze. His large body came closer, lowering until his heat seared her. Another thigh moved between hers, spreading her legs. Each and every sensation built and magnified. Cream seemed to pour from within her in a way she'd never imagined possible.

"I want to be inside you," he whispered hotly against her neck, even as he kept his hips away from hers. She searched for his cock, wanting him to fill her like he'd done before. His shaft was already aroused again and as she massaged its length, it began to harden even more. She stared at it in wonder, amazed by his quick recovery.

"James, please," she begged.

"Do you want me?" His very touch made her want to bend to his will, not that she ever thought of denying him.

"Yes," she panted, closing her eyes.

"How do you want me?"

At that, she opened her eyes. Passion burned within her but she wasn't one for vocalizing what she wanted. In fact, none of her very limited past lovers had ever asked her what she wanted. James looked like a reined beast, struggling for control. His boldness excited her, as did his confidence. She wanted this, wanted him.

"How?" he repeated.

"I want you to...fuck me." She tried not to hesitate when she said it but her voice wavered. James merely smiled, kissing the corner of her mouth. "I want to feel you inside me."

Her pussy ached, desperate for contact. James lowered his chin, lightly kissing her breast. "That will do for now."

Claudia spread her legs, ready to be dominated. His large size didn't frighten her as much as the first time. She wanted him to fuck her. His cock brushed her thigh and she tensed, sure he'd give it to her. Instead he worked down her stomach, rimming her navel before dipping between her legs. He nibbled the flesh of her inner thigh, making his way to the soft thatch of glistening curls guarding her sex. She looked down, meeting his eyes, and watched as he flicked his tongue toward her clit. Deep inside, she knew he wanted her to watch. The knowledge seemed a clear thought connecting them in a flash of transparency.

Gasping, she tensed as he discovered her with his mouth. His warm tongue stroked her, working along her folds, twirling around her clit. She pushed up from the bed, watching his head between her legs, mesmerized by the beauty of his form. She felt his desire, his every motion—in the way his eyes took her in, the way his mouth curled at the sight in contentment. Somewhere, in the fog of her building need, she heard her own voice begging for more, saying things she'd never before voiced in such moments of lust. She squirmed, clamping down tight against his head, but he only forced her legs farther apart. He growled, making her pussy vibrate with the raspy breath. It was too much, felt too good. The tension built and she came with a jolt. The intense shock waves flowed over her in a cascading rush of extreme pleasure. He groaned, noisily lapping up her cream.

Claudia was still breathing hard, her heart hammering in her chest, when he lifted himself above her. His full, erect cock again brushed along her thigh, but this time it kept coming at her, finding her wet, trembling center. His penis brushed against her slit and she cried out. She'd just come but her need for him to fill her was more urgent than before. He pushed, entering her, stretching her body wide. She gasped, the sensation more stunning than anything she'd ever experienced.

She held on to his shoulders. James worked in shallow thrusts, letting her adjust to his size. Then her body loosened, accepting him with ease. His hands braced on the bed, holding his weight. Their bodies strained toward each other, moving in perfect unison. The force of his claim drove her body up on the bed, sliding her back with each plunge.

James' eyes glowed more than before, the brown completely replaced by the amber color. When he opened his mouth, fangs protruded from his gums. Somehow the sight of his beast pushed her over the edge again. She tensed, her orgasm hitting hard as he brought his mouth down. To her surprise, he bit her and his teeth sank into the flesh of her neck. For a brief moment of complete clarity, she felt as if she saw inside him, heard his thoughts. The instant was over so fast, she didn't have time to memorize what she'd seen and the sensations slipped away before she could grab hold. With pleasure and pain drawing a course through her at the same time, she couldn't concentrate, didn't think to fight it. The perfection of the moment became too much. Darkness consumed her and she fell into it, drifting into a dreamless sleep.

8

Claudia opened her eyes. She was naked on the bed but James was gone. A dull ache radiated over her muscles but it wasn't enough to keep her in bed. Pushing up, she stretched her arms toward the ceiling. Suddenly the door opened behind her and she spun, covering her naked breasts with her arm as she automatically fumbled for the blanket to hide her nudity.

Sunlight illuminated James from behind, giving a golden firelight effect to his brown hair and shadowing his face. She blinked several times, having been away from the sunlight for a while, awakening only at night. A cool breeze drifted in, bringing with it a hint of bacon and ham. More meat. Even as her mind frowned at the idea, her stomach growled, loud and long.

James laughed, shutting the door behind him. He set the bag on the table. "I'm pleased to see you are up. I brought breakfast. After we eat, we should get on the road. I'd like to make it to Atlantic City by tonight and I must admit the drive will go easier with someone to talk to."

"I'm assuming this is the next morning? Not a month later?" The same room she'd woken up to earlier now surrounded her.

"Yes, it is the next morning. I'm glad to see you are awake. It's a good sign." He opened the bag and began pulling out cartons of food, laying napkins and plastic forks next to them.

"A good sign of what?" Claudia glanced around, seeing her shirt on the floor. Grabbing it, she pulled it over her head. Next, she slipped on the pajama pants.

"That you are getting better."

She detected that he hid something from her in his too-easy tone. "Can I ask you something?"

He arched a brow.

"Yeah, stupid question, sorry." Claudia walked toward him. "Where do you live?"

He chuckled. "Out of hotels. Occasionally I'll crash at one of my brothers' houses."

"You don't have a home of your own?" she asked in surprise.

"No, not really. Since I'm a tracker for our lycan clan, I keep moving around too much to settle in one place." He shrugged. "Actually I might have a few homes but I can't remember if I sold them or not."

Claudia sat down at the table. "What do you mean, you can't remember? How can you not remember selling a house?"

James took a deep breath, studying his hands. "I'm older than you might think me. Along with being a lycan, we're granted a very long life. It's part of our genetic makeup. Our cells regenerate, healing wounds and illnesses, keeping us strong and in," he paused, glancing down his chest mischievously, "perfect physical shape. With more years comes more time to learn."

"How many years are we talking about? Hundred and fifty? Two hundred?"

James jerked his thumb toward the ceiling, indicating more.

"Three? Four hundred?"

"Let's just say I have vague memories from the Middle Ages." He grabbed a piece of bacon, biting into it. Pointing at her, he said, "This doesn't work as good as the steak but I love it."

Claudia was less enthusiastic. "How long will I be on this protein diet?"

"A few months." He wiggled the bacon in her direction. The words *If you live past your first shift* hung unspoken between them. Claudia forced a weak smile, hoping to keep the moment light.

"Because I really, *really* like eating carbs," she grumbled, taking a piece of bacon from him and biting into it.

9

JAMES WASN'T JOKING when he said they had a long drive. Imagining him to be centuries old became a little too incredible, so she focused on the fact that he looked like a man in his mid-thirties. He allowed for minimal stops, once to order an obscene amount of plain hamburgers from which he took away the buns, another time they stopped for a restroom break and another still for fuel and drinks.

After they'd eaten, she felt the fire burning inside her and couldn't help but move closer to him on the seat. But who was she kidding? She felt the burning desire without the aid of protein. The meat was only an excuse. One look at him and she had to have him.

First, she kissed his neck, eliciting deep, sexy moans. Soon her kisses traveled down, sprinkling across his stomach while she lifted his shirt before finally settling around the cock jutting from his opened pants. She'd never given head in a moving car before but the erotic magnetism of James' body was too much to resist. But it was more than his body. It was the look in his eyes, the sound of his voice, the smell of his hair. They all made her want him.

The thick length of his cock nearly choked her as she sucked. James' hand rested firmly on the back of her head, pressing down. She felt the car swerve a few times but he didn't run it off the road. A passing car honked and some man on a motorcycle screamed in approval. He came hard, grunting and breathing heavily. She drank him down, moaning softly. Wiping her lips, she sat back in the seat, highly aroused.

"You amaze me," James whispered, reaching to cup her cheek.

The tender expression on his face made her heart melt. How did this happen? How did she find him? And how was it she felt as if she knew him better than she knew herself? "I amaze myself sometimes." She smiled back at him and their eyes held each other for a few seconds.

Claudia felt her heart leap in her chest. Her feelings tried to rush forth in words, desperate to proclaim her emotions in bold declarations of love and desire. She held back, not trusting herself. With all that was happening, how could she know what she felt was real? So instead she gave him another small smile and lowered her lashes seductively over her eyes, letting him see by their expression how much she wanted him.

He pulled off the main road just long enough to fuck her against the hood of his car. His nails bit into her ass as he bent her over and lifted her skirt. Hard, hot metal pressed into her chest through the dress. The thick, pounding shaft entered her from behind and she surrendered to him as he expertly brought her to climax.

The New Jersey landscape drew the eye, especially when they reached the shoreline. Peeks of the Atlantic Ocean from the roadway captured her attention. The smell of cool, salty air swept through the rolled-down windows of the rental car—a small sedan with tan interior and leather seats that stuck uncomfortably to the backs of her legs. To her surprise, James had bought not only pajamas for her but dresses as well. The loose material hung around her frame in a one-size-fits-all sort of way. The tiny flower print was very feminine and unlike anything she owned in her closet. Her tastes generally leaned toward jeans, tank tops and a sizable collection of rock band t-shirts.

At first, James held pleasant conversation, talking about everything from his favorite music to his many travels. He'd been to every country in the world at least once. She loved listening to his voice, the way his eyes lit up when he spoke, how his hands lifted from the steering wheel to emphasize the meaning. He often looked her in the eye, glancing at her as he drove.

Her obvious desire and affection for him became a true liking the more lucid her thoughts became. The man was funny, smart, if not a little serious at times, but she imagined the nature of his job— hunting bad people just like a federal marshal or police detective—might make him overly somber.

As they drove, a worry line developed between his eyes, causing him to look less and less at her and more at the distant road. Signs for Atlantic City were everywhere and by evening, they were pulling into the bright city.

"How will you find her here?" Claudia asked, looking around at the tall hotels and numerous casinos. Signs along the streets boasted gourmet food, fishing, golf, water sports, top-notch entertainment, full-service spas, endless shopping and every casino game known to man. How would they ever find one person in such a big city?

James didn't answer but instead grabbed his phone. Pushing a couple of buttons, he held it to his ear. "Yeah, we're here. Just pulled into town."

Claudia tried to hear the other side of the conversation without being obvious.

"Ian's made it? Is Ceana with him? Great." James glanced at her. Claudia kept her eyes forward, pretending to look at the passing sights. "I agree she should stay with Natasha."

"This is no place for a woman. I requested the king send someone to stay with your charge but he is insistent you're the only one to help her," a voice answered. The words were faint as if on the other side of a tunnel but the more Claudia concentrated, the more she could understand. Her hearing had become better than before. The man on the phone continued, "The truth is he hasn't told the others about her and the family has been sworn to secrecy until it can be determined whether or not her first full moon will kill her."

Claudia gasped to hear her fate talked about so casually. Her eyes rounded, instantly giving away that she'd been eavesdropping.

"Damn it, Roark," James swore.

"Shit, she can hear me? Why didn't you say so? I figured you were in a secure area if you called me about this," Roark answered.

"Apparently her hearing is better than I'd realized. She's developing quickly." James looked at her briefly before watching the road.

"That's good, right? Um, Claudia, that's good. I was just being dramatic. Sorry about what I said. Really, there isn't anything to worry about," Roark said, still talking to his brother but aware she could hear him.

"That's all..." Her whisper trailed off.

"Don't panic," James said to her, his voice strained. Then he addressed his brother. "I told her of our kind and of her imminent turning with the first full moon."

"You told her everything?" She couldn't be sure but Roark sounded skeptical. "Can she link yet?"

"Link?" Claudia asked.

"Where is Meghan, Roark?" James' hard voice was curt. He didn't answer her.

"Lavette Spa and Casino. It's the newest hotel along the Boardwalk. Just look for the pink glow lighting up the building. You can't miss it," Roark said. "I've already booked you a suite next to mine and Ian and Randall are bunking with me. Just ask the front desk for a key."

"Thanks, I'll be there soon." James hung up the phone.

Claudia swallowed nervously. All the appeal of the surrounding buildings paled in comparison to what she'd just heard. Somehow she'd believed that everything would be fine, that James would protect her. Strange, since she didn't really know him for all that long. But to hear Roark talk about her death made it all the more real. Nerves tightened her gut as the gravity of her situation bore down on her. She might only have a little over a week to live. And if she did survive, what then? Eternity as a wolf, craving blood and sex?

The sex part won't be so bad. She glanced at James, the beginning of her smile fading into a frown. But what if he was only with her because he thought she was dying?

"Claudia," James began.

"I know you said the full moon was the final test, but what are the odds that I'll make it?" Claudia shivered. She imagined this was much like when someone heard they might have only a few days to live. Her nose began to burn with unshed tears. Maybe it wasn't as much of a risk as she feared.

"Only a very few make it through the shift. It is why we don't try to turn humans. There is no way of telling which of you will make the change or why those that do can survive it." James' hand lifted as if he wanted to reach for her. "I didn't tell you of the odds because I didn't want you to worry."

"What else haven't you told me?" she asked.

"Nothing that couldn't be explained after your transformation. Things that would only burden your thoughts before it was necessary to do so."

"Ow!" Claudia grabbed her temple.

"What?"

"I don't know. This shooting pain in my head." She took a deep breath, suddenly nauseous. "Do you smell fish?"

"We are by the sea," he said.

"No, not that, like cooking fish." She closed her eyes tight. "And laughter. Glasses are tinkling like someone's toasting champagne. You can't hear that?"

"Do you see anything?" James probed.

"No, just sounds." Claudia opened her eyes. "Why? What is it?"

"Meghan is definitely close. Since you were bitten by her, you are connected to her. I didn't know it would happen so soon but, perhaps because of your psychic heritage, it is occurring sooner." He gave her an expectant look. "Can you find her? Did you detect her saying anything? Feel where she was or what she was thinking? Do you think she detected you?" There was desperation in his eyes when he questioned her.

"I don't know. It happened too fast." Claudia took deep breaths. "I think this counts as something you should have told me."

Despite all of what James might feel for her as a lover, perhaps even as a friend, she was a means to capturing his prey—a prey that had eluded him so far. That was the real reason she was with him. Her connection to Meghan would help him find the killer.

"Here's the hotel." James turned the car up a wide drive. "We'll pick up our keys and get you into the suite. Maybe you'll pick up more details there."

"I need a drink," Claudia said, never having uttered those words in her life. But, if ever she was going to start consuming alcohol, now seemed like a great time. She pressed against her throbbing temple. "A really big one."

THE NEWLY BUILT Lavette Spa and Casino had every state-of-the-art comfort possible in a hotel, from a health club and Olympic-sized pool to steam baths and tanning beds. Grand chandeliers, their sparkling crystals glittering like stars, lined the gold-crested ceilings. Lights sparkled over the floor, dancing on the ornate Italianate marble like tiny fairies.

Costumed dancers and uniformed staff assimilated in the building like fine-tuned entities, there to smile and serve. Claudia couldn't muster much of a smile to greet them in return and kept her eyes on the valet's back as he pushed their meager luggage toward the hotel's elevator.

"Would the lady like me to arrange a spa treatment for her?" the valet asked, his tone even and polite.

"No," Claudia said, even as James answered in kind. "No."

The valet chuckled. The elevator stopped on the forty-third floor before opening. "Mr. O'Connell, I've been instructed to inform you that your brothers are in the adjoining suite. You can reach them through the private-door access." The valet opened a wide door, allowing them entry into the suite.

"This room is expensive, isn't it?" James said under his breath. "Trust Roark to pick it. I hope he knows he's paying."

Claudia briefly thought about offering to pay for some of the cost but kept her mouth shut. She didn't want to think about money at a time like this.

"The suites offer the best accommodations in the city," the valet answered. "Room service is open all night, as are the eight restaurants found on the main level. The spa is on level three."

"Thank you." James slipped the valet a folded bill, tipping him. "But we don't want to be disturbed. At all."

"Very good, Mr. O'Connell," the valet answered, grinning knowingly.

When they were alone, Claudia walked into the

center of the large suite. Creams and chocolate browns covered every surface that wasn't wood. Over one thousand square feet, the suite had a furnished bar, couches and big-screen television, all set before floor-to-ceiling glass doors. Crossing over to them, she pushed the doors open and stepped out on the balcony. Ocean-scented air accosted her senses and she took a deep, steadying breath. Evening had turned to night during check-in and now she was surrounded by the stars and sounds of the waves below.

"I'm sorry you heard Roark's words. He didn't mean to sound so harsh about the shift." James joined her, standing close as he leaned against the metal railing next to her. He put a gentle hand on her shoulder. "I need you to try to sense Meghan again."

"I don't know if I can." Claudia swallowed nervously. She wasn't sure she wanted to.

"You must try. Your connection might be our best shot at finding her before she harms anyone else."

"Is this why you kept me with you?" Claudia knew enough from her mother to know what to do to encourage visions, but she wanted answers first. "Is this why you were nice to me? To get me to sense your runaway?"

"I was nice to you because I want to be." He ran a

frustrated hand through his hair, sighing heavily. "I'll admit, the idea did cross my mind about you being able to help us, but I would have helped you either way."

"Because it's your duty to do so?"

"Yes," he cleared his throat, "and no."

Her breath coming in hard rasps, she licked her lips, longing to kiss him. This time she hadn't eaten and she knew what she was feeling was of her own doing—not protein or some changing. She wanted him for him, needed him, desired him. Her stomach tightened and cream flooded her pussy with a disarming suddenness. Heat infused her cheeks and neck, curling a haphazard path over her entire body.

As if he could sense what she felt, he came to her. "Come inside the room."

She did, following him in. His hand caressed her flushed cheek. She closed her eyes tight, not moving as his fingers ran down the length of her throat. Her heart beat wildly, in hard, heavy thumps against her chest.

Claudia bit her lip as James began to undress her and didn't let it go for a long time. The feel of material sliding off her body was erotic in itself. His harsh breathing joined hers as he teased her flesh by denying it his fingers. When she stood naked, she still hadn't opened her eyes. She couldn't. The feelings were too much, swirling inside her. If she looked, she might profess a love he didn't want or need to hear about. There was so much to be done first. Meghan had to be stopped. She had to face her first full moon. And then there was the small fear that he might not feel as deeply for her as she felt for him. She hated the insecurity but she couldn't suppress it. She'd never wanted anyone so much and the mere thought that he might not feel the same tore at her chest.

"Look at me," James said, his tone low.

How could she not obey when he asked her like that, all gentle and husky? She did, unable to keep from staring. While she had kept her eyes closed, he'd taken off his clothes and now stood naked and proud before her. Without pants, there was nothing to hide the protruding erection from view. The huge cock, thick and straining with veins along the wide shaft, towered from his thighs above the soft globes of his balls.

Her sex wept with the memory of how deeply he could penetrate her and her mouth watered to take him in. James walked toward her, causing her to back up until she was near the bed. Not touching her, he leaned forward. Claudia fell back, shivering at the intensity in him. He'd never proceeded this slowly, never looked at her with such penetrating eyes. It was as if he could read her very soul.

He took the back of his hand and ran it down her flesh, tracing a light trail down the valley of her breasts, over her navel, to rest above her slick pussy. Instinctively her legs parted and her head rolled back on the bed while she arched, offering herself to him. Turning his hand toward her, he cupped her sex and parted the wet folds with a probing finger. It wasn't long before he discovered her clit and rubbed it mercilessly. She moaned and writhed. Her hands gripped tight over her head as she held on to the stiff coverlet beneath her.

James let loose an animalistic noise of pleasure. The finger became more insistent, delving inside the damp heat of her cavern. The look of him above her, each muscle pulled tight, caused her to moan. "I need you, James, please. I want to feel you inside me. I want you to kiss me."

"How can I deny such a pretty plea?" He stared at her mouth in a way that made her weak.

Parting her lips, she watched him crawl completely over her, his legs slipping between her thighs to keep them open. He brushed his mouth to hers, teasing mercilessly several times before finally taking her fully. James groaned and she swallowed the sound. Their lips warred, moving at a more frantic pace with each second. She sucked his tongue hard, pulling it deep into her mouth. Finally, needing breath, she pulled back and gasped for air.

James grabbed her by the hip and pushed her thighs wider as he drew himself up between them. His confident movements made the ache for him all that much worse. His heat burnt into her sensitive thighs as he rocked forward, using her leg as a guide to reach her ready sex.

She couldn't take it anymore. Claudia had to touch him. She ran her hands down his chest, scratching and kneading as she begged, "Yes, please, James. Do it. Fuck me. I need you so badly it hurts. Please..."

Her words became a mumbling mass of pleas as she squirmed. A warm palm grabbed her breast, pinching an already-tight nipple. The jolt of pleasure rocketing to her pussy made her gasp. She lurched forward, unable to take any more as she flipped him onto his back with a strength she didn't know she possessed. The soft hairs on his legs grazed her sensitive thighs and she could tell he fought his body's shifting. He'd teased her to the point of madness and she needed the torment to end.

His nostrils flared as she moved above him, as if

he could smell her arousal. He grabbed on to her hips, holding her steady. The thick length of his cock heaved in excitement as she brought herself down on him. Pushing up, he met her movement, filling her much faster and deeper than she had expected.

Claudia held still, enjoying the feel of his cock as her flexing muscles formed around him, accepting him, molding her tightened, silk depths to fit only him. The animal growing inside her took over. She lifted up only to slam down hard, taking his turgid shaft with her tight sex. Her body hummed with passion. She had never wanted anyone or anything as badly as she wanted him.

She dug her fingers into his chest, using them as leverage as she rode him hard, their bodies banging together. His eyes glowed with supernatural force. Claudia drew a deeply ragged breath. She saw her own breasts thrust forward, bobbing wantonly with each pounding thrust. She cried out, desperate for completion, and she thought she might explode with the need for climax.

Suddenly James grunted. Her pussy convulsed, gripping his cock tight. The tension was more than she could take. Her orgasm hit her and she released so hard she jerked violently on top of him. Only his hands on her hips kept her from falling over. James' body answered her call, jutting the hot stream of his cum deep inside her willing pussy. Claudia collapsed on his chest, sliding to the side, so weak she couldn't move. They held each other close in stunned silence.

As the tiny, remaining spasms slowly subsided, she opened her mouth to speak. But all words of love left her as a sudden, intense pain shot through her head. Claudia screamed, grabbing her temples on both sides. She squeezed hard, pushing in to get the sensation to stop. Her mother and grandmother had never experienced such pain when they had a vision. The blinding headache spread, turning her vision to a bright white until everything was blocked out by it. "Argh!"

"What do you see?" James demanded, pushing up on the bed. His arms wrapped around her, trying to give comfort.

"I see her," Claudia said, getting a clear vision of the woman from the Block Island beach. Even though her eyes were open, her sight was replaced by the image in her mind. It was as if she watched through someone else's eyes. "She's watching dancers. A show. Red costumes. Sparkles. Feathers. Smoke. I smell liquor."

"What else?"

"She's in the hotel. Her napkin reads *Lavette Spa*

and Casino. A man is with her. Long brown hair, firelight in his eyes." Claudia sensed the evil in the lycan woman, the taste for blood, the deep craving for it—so much so that she felt sick after experiencing the secondhand feelings. She shook her head back and forth, trying to get rid of the picture. It worked. The scene faded, replaced by what was actually in front of her eyes. "You had better hurry. I have the sense that they will be leaving soon."

"Claudia." James touched her cheek. "I have to do this. Please stay in this room. Don't let anyone in, not even room service."

Claudia nodded. James stood and she heard the sound of him shuffling to pull on his clothes. She followed more slowly, not really paying attention to what she put on. She was too busy watching James. When they were fully dressed, he went to a private door. He glanced at her to double-check she had all her clothes on. Claudia quickly rearranged the bed and nodded to him. James opened the private door to a second, closed one. He knocked and it didn't take long before the sound was answered. The man could only be James' brother.

"Roark," James said in greeting, confirming her deduction as he gave the man a hug. The two brothers had the same look to them, though Roark was slightly smaller in stature and had waist-length, dark brown hair. His leather pants and tight crimson shirt gave him the air of a rock star.

"Yeah, yeah, I already know you. Where's the girl?" Roark asked cheerfully. His dark eyes fell on her and his grin widened. "Ah, there she is! Welcome to the clan, Claudia!"

James looked into the other suite, "Where's Ian?"

"Downstairs scouting," Roark answered. Claudia stood still, frozen in place as the enthusiastic man came for her. His arms spread wide and she stumbled back from him. Roark stopped, his smile fading as he looked at his brother.

"She's scared of me?" Roark asked. "I thought you told her about us."

"I did." James looked at Claudia. "What is it?"

"He was with Meghan. Long brown hair. I felt the same feeling I do now." Claudia continued to back away. Though she did not recognize his face from her vision, the feeling she had was unmistakable and overwhelming.

"What?" Roark gave a small laugh. "She's joking, right?"

"I don't believe so," James said. Then, to Claudia, he insisted, "You have to be mistaken. Roark would never conspire with Meghan. Besides, you just had the vision. Roark couldn't have made it here so fast."

Claudia looked from brother to brother, still not trusting Roark. Unconvinced, she whispered, "If you're certain."

♣

JAMES LOOKED from Claudia to his brother. There was much he wanted to say to her but right now he had more pressing concerns. Besides, what could he tell her? There was something in her eyes that told him she no longer blindly trusted his words. The truth was, he had been surprised she'd trusted him so readily before.

"I swear to you, Roark is a friend, Claudia," James insisted. "Your feelings must be confused. Either that or you felt him as one of the clan. You can trust him."

When Claudia looked at him, he felt as if he'd been kicked. "I'm not sure I can trust that. I know what I felt." She shook her head. "And at the same time I'm not sure what I felt."

"Jame—" Roark began.

James recognized the teasing in his brother's tone

and instantly stopped him from continuing. "No, Roark, now isn't the time."

"You're right." Claudia lifted her chin, her eyes narrowing as she rubbed her temple. He wanted to go to her, to soothe the obvious headache starting anew. "Now is not the time. She's preparing to leave the show. If you wish to stop Meghan from killing again, now is it. Meghan drinks in a bar or restaurant with another like her. Dancers in red Vegas-showgirl-style costumes are sauntering around, kicking their legs in time with fast music." She met James' gaze. "She's picked her victim—a hooker in a black slinky dress and too-red lipstick. When the woman leaves, they plan to follow her."

James knew what he had to do but a large part of him wanted to stay with Claudia, to comfort her, help her and convince her that he was worth trusting.

James? Roark said through their mind-link. *She is right. We need to capture Meghan.*

She's still upset, James answered.

Deal with your lover later, after the threat is gone. I'm sorry, brother, but if she doesn't make it, we'll lose our only link to Meghan and if we don't go now, the bitch is sure to kill again.

James nodded. *Meet me in the hall.*

Be quick. Roark left through the door to his own suite.

"You should get going," Claudia said. "I know how important her capture is to you."

"We'll talk when I get back. Don't open the door unless you hear me knock three times and tell you my name." James didn't want to leave her like this. Why hadn't he talked to her in the car after hanging up with Roark or before they'd made love? Even as he wondered, he knew the answer. It was the same reason he didn't say the right thing now. He wasn't sure what the right thing was.

Claudia nodded. "Good luck finding her."

"She smells of you," Roark eyed James from across the elevator. It had taken them ten minutes to get one to stop on their floor that had enough room to carry them down. Oddly, when a free elevator finally came, it was empty and they were left alone. "Though she doesn't seem too charmed by you at the moment. I told you that you were too serious. You need to loosen up, show her the fun side of James—if you have one. Do you have a fun side, James?"

"This elevator has security cameras," James answered, motioning up. "You should be quiet. Someone can probably hear you and I won't stop them if they try to have you thrown into an asylum."

"Do they even use asylums anymore? Isn't there a more politically correct term for them now?" Roark chuckled. "I might have done the same in your position if a pretty little thing like that attacked me in lust during her changing. Did the kitty have claws?"

"Leave me be," James grumbled.

"I take it you have not told the king about claiming a woman for your own?" Roark continued.

"Don't make me tell your mate what you are saying." James gave a small smile when Roark snapped his mouth shut. The elevator dinged and opened, ending all conversation. People stepped on for the ride down and all became quiet. When they finally reached their stop, the doors opened, revealing the first floor.

"Ian should be down here already watching for her." Roark pulled out his phone. "I'll call him. I don't want Meghan detecting our thoughts. There are several restaurants and clubs along the north side. I'll look there for dancers in red. You check the other side."

James glanced up at the high ceiling, to where Claudia waited in the suite. He'd ordered her to lock all doors and not do anything that would require her opening them—like calling the hotel staff or room service. Hopefully Meghan would be too busy fighting him and his brothers to hunt or even detect a turning human in the middle of a fifty-story hotel.

Roark took off across the lobby. James moved in the opposite direction. He heard music and laughter, the kind often associated with bars. This had to be it. Tonight would be the night he caught Meghan and ended her reign of terror forever.

Claudia paced the floor, debating whether or not she should stay in the posh suite doing nothing. She didn't trust Roark, though the fact that he was James' brother caused her to doubt her judgment. The feeling she got when he was near was too familiar to the sensation she'd gotten when she'd had access to Meghan's mind.

Working alone all day with computers didn't exactly create a superhero. However, if she only had a few days to live, she was going to do something with those days. At first, she'd considered running away from the whole lycan thing, but when she thought of James, of his touch, she couldn't do it. If these were to be her last days, they'd have meaning.

Besides, who was she kidding? She couldn't leave James, no matter the circumstances. Too much of her heart was wrapped up in him and that scared her. What if he didn't feel the same way? They never talked about such emotions.

She tried to watch television but her mind couldn't concentrate. Then she tried to focus on Meghan to see what the woman was doing, hoping for some kind of hint as to what happened downstairs when the brothers confronted her.

No matter how she tried, she couldn't get a link to Meghan's thoughts. Suddenly three knocks sounded on the door. Claudia jumped, instantly recognizing James' signal. Crossing to the door, she hesitated. "Yes?"

"It's Prince Ian, James' other brother. He sent me to check in on you," a voice from the other side said.

Claudia reached for the lock, only to pause. "Where's James?"

"In the lobby with Roark. He said to tell you he sent me and to knock three times. Can I come in?" Claudia glanced at the door adjoining her room to the brothers' suite, wondering why he didn't come through that door instead. "All right."

Claudia pulled open the door slowly. The man in

the hall had the same features as James, with dark eyes and long hair that looked very much like Roark's. He smiled, a charming, easy expression as he stepped inside.

"Did you say you were a prince?" she asked. "Or is prince your first name?"

"He hasn't told you?" Ian chuckled. "We're all three of us princes—James, Roark and I. Though I am the oldest and next in line to rule."

"A prince?" Claudia gave him a skeptical look, sure he was messing with her. "Right."

"I can see why James is taken with you." Ian reached for her face. Claudia stiffened until she realized he only meant to kiss her cheek. Brushing his lips against her, he paused, taking a deep breath. "My apologies. James is more than taken with you. He's laid claim to you."

Claudia reached for her neck, where James had bitten her while they had sex. She wondered at the strange look Ian gave her. "I'd offer you a drink but I don't want to run up James' bill." She put distance between them, slowly making her way across the room.

Ian laughed. "His family is richer than a sultan and still he lives like a man on a budget."

"Well..." Claudia began to defend James.

Ian chuckled harder. "I have a drink in my room. Be right back."

Claudia nodded, for some reason feeling sick to her stomach. "All right."

Ian unlocked the door to his suite, stopping to look at her. "He will defiantly be very sorry to lose you."

That shocked her and her mouth worked several times before she managed to say, "Ah, I suppose. But we haven't spoken of it. I have a week before the full moon."

"Oh, he wasn't talking about your transformation," a female voice said from inside Ian's suite. "He was talking about James losing you tonight."

"Meghan," Claudia whispered, knowing who was inside as sure as she knew her own heartbeat. Her nerve endings tingled, pulled toward where the woman appeared in the door. On Block Island, she didn't have time to see her attacker fully before getting abducted. Meghan's evilness marred her perfect beauty. Her amber eyes, darkened with eyeliner, glowed with all the mysterious power of lycan and woman. Silky smooth, jet-black hair fell around her shoulders, framing her full, red lips and oval face.

Meghan laughed. "Hi, little one. Mommy's home!"

"Ian?" Claudia looked at James' brother.

"Sorry, not Ian." Meghan pretended to pout. "Randall O'Connell, did you tell Claudia you were a prince? Shame on you. Tell her the truth. She should know how easily you duped James into believing you tracked me for him. Tell her how we laughed as you called to report on me from my bed."

"Randall?" Claudia shivered. He wasn't James' brother?

"I am your prince," Randall answered, trying to slip his arm around Meghan's waist. She dodged his advance, coming toward Claudia.

"You are the one I sensed with her, aren't you? It wasn't Roark," Claudia said.

"That's the O'Connell clan you're sensing. They all feel the same, don't they?" Meghan giggled.

James, come back. Please come back. Claudia bit the inside of her lip, trying to force a calm expression to her features.

"Oh, sweetheart," Meghan shook her head, clucking her tongue in mock concern. "Your mind-link isn't developed. James can't hear you yet. But I can. How do you think I knew about the three knocks to get in? I'll admit, I can't see everything but I see more than enough in your mind. You're not very guarded, but one can't expect control from one so young. And I must thank you, my daughter, for sending me those helpful images of where you were. Of course you didn't know you were doing it, but thanks all the same. You make it very easy to elude capture. Almost too easy. There was no fun in being chased when you know where your pursuer is at all times."

"But tonight you will have fun, won't you, darling? I mean, that's why you allowed the brothers to find you. To show them how powerful you are and elude them again." Randall tried to put his arms around Meghan, this time from behind. She rolled her eyes in annoyance, making sure though that he could not see her expression.

James! Claudia couldn't help her thoughts. *James, please come back to the room. Come back.*

"Stop it!" Meghan yelled, her face twisting into a snarl. "Quit calling for him. He won't come to save you." Then, regaining her composure, she took a deep breath, again smiling. "Oh, Claudia, don't look so worried. I'm here to take care of you. I can smell he's laid claim to you, but was that really fair of him? In your condition? You should at least have options between your thighs before you commit to one lycan."

"Laid claim? I don't know what you mean but I won't help you. That's why you're here, isn't it?" Claudia tried to inch away from the woman, keeping the door to the hallway in her peripheral line of sight.

"Ah, sweetie, you don't really have a choice. You're mine. I made you." Meghan's eyes narrowed. "And you are going to continue to help me. I don't need your permission or even your willingness."

Claudia made a run for the door but Meghan was too fast. She darted in front of her, blocking the way.

"I was going to let you live initially, but now that James has laid his mark on you, I think this will be the best purpose to your new life. Let him wonder if you would have survived the changing. When I kill you, James will know he failed." Meghan laughed. Randall moved to block the door leading to the adjoining suite. "Let him know he failed again."

"You will be brought to justice," Claudia said, though she wasn't sure it was the truth.

"Oh, isn't she adorable, Randall? So innocent. I almost hate to get rid of her." Meghan shook her head as if disappointed.

"We could keep her. Turn her to our cause. There is no need to kill her," Randall said.

"She'll never join us. I can see too much of her spirit, all good and light. It makes me sick to even feel her. I'd kill her just to get those feelings out of my body." Meghan visibly shivered.

Claudia looked at Randall in hope of salvation, but those thoughts were soon crushed when Meghan answered, "Do you want to fuck her so badly, Randy? Maybe if you beg me, I'll let you stick it to her."

Randall shook his head in denial. "The princes will already seek my head for my betrayal. I'll not desecrate their woman and add to my crime."

"You still fear them? You should fear your queen," Meghan spat out.

"I worship you, you know that," Randall argued, "but..."

Claudia ran for the balcony, the only other exit in the hotel room. She wasn't sure if there would be a way to climb down or even over to the next room, but she had to try. To stay would mean her death and she wasn't ready to go. Not yet. If what they said was true, if James had somehow laid claim to her in a way the other lycans could tell just by being near her, than she had a big reason to live. Maybe he did care for her more than just a lover. Maybe there was hope. Her heart told her there was.

"Bitch!" Meghan screamed.

Claudia heard footsteps pounding on the carpet behind her. Blood pumped in her veins, filling her with desperation and fear. She grabbed on to the glass door, jerking it open so she could get onto the balcony. But her plan for flight wasn't well thought-out and she ended up closing a door she couldn't lock from the outside.

The glass was no match for Meghan's fists. The woman's face shifted and Claudia screamed. Fangs grew from Meghan's mouth as her nose elongated. Fur sprouted by her eyes and the morbid sound of bones breaking punctuated the air. The lycan woman fell forward, her flesh rippling as she completely changed into a large wolf.

Claudia had known what lycans were, but to see it for the first time nearly made her heart stop. Instead of landing on all fours on the concrete balcony, Meghan landed on Claudia. Claws dug into Claudia's arms, ripping her flesh. Instantly, she lost her footing and stumbled back, surprised by the lycan's massive weight. She pushed Meghan to get her to let go but, as her back hit the railing, she knew it was too late.

Her body flipped over the side. Meghan's claws let loose and the night was pierced with her evil laughter. Bloody images filled Claudia's head as the wind rushed past her head. As she fell, her flesh prickled as if thousands of glass shards passed through her. The bloody visions left her, only to be replaced by one that was much worse—the look of the sidewalk speeding toward her plummeting body.

OH, *lover boy*, Meghan's voice echoed in his mind. The taunt was followed by a graphic image of Claudia falling from the high-story balcony.

"Claudia," James gasped, feeling a rush of fear rippling through him. As suddenly as it came, it disappeared, leaving an emptiness so terrifying he thought he was dead. He looked at his brothers. The elevator seemed to go too slow but he couldn't make it climb to his suite's floor any faster. He and his brothers had gotten on it only seconds after James felt Claudia call to him in fear, begging him to come back to the room, to save her. He tried to answer but had no way of knowing if she could hear him. Grabbing his chest, he panted for breath.

"What is it?" Ian demanded. His dark brown,

shoulder-length hair was pulled back to the nape of his neck and he wore a lightweight sweater and leather jacket. "What happened?"

"James, are you well? You look as if you've been stabbed," Roark added, getting hold of his arm.

"Meghan pushed..." James couldn't say the words. "I have to get to the lobby."

"Meghan pushed who?" Ian began, only to have his face drain of color. "No, she wouldn't. It's some kind of trick."

"I can't feel her," James said.

"Meghan would want to torture you first. Pushing someone from a balcony wouldn't be much fun for a woman like her," Roark said, though he didn't look convinced.

James didn't find his words comforting. His skin prickled as his body threatened to shift and this time he wasn't sure if he'd be able to hold back the beast inside him. Breathing hard, he bit his lip, trying to control the violent rage clouding his vision with thoughts of blood.

When the elevator door opened, he took off running. Meghan wouldn't have had time to escape the suite. A mortal woman screamed as he tore down the hall, breaking the door to his room. He heard his brothers open their own door. The sounds of a battle ensued from Roark's suite.

Randall, you traitor! Ian's voice yelled in his mind.

Two lycans stood in his room, their bodies stiff as they blocked Meghan behind them. James vaguely recognized them as being from the disbanded Douglass clan. The man from the boat who'd helped Meghan escape Block Island was one of them. He tried to detect Claudia but didn't sense her in the room.

The two were strong but their power was no match for James' rage and fear. Leaping forward, he partially shifted. Claws bit into his chest and side but James kept going, breaking the neck of the first man and clawing open an artery of the second. Blood squirted over the suite but James continued. Meghan screamed, her eyes rounding in fear, and he knew she'd underestimated him greatly.

"James, wait, please," Meghan began, holding up her hands. Her naked body and the nearby pile of shredded clothes attested to a recent shift. Though physically beautiful, she did not tempt him. Compared to Claudia, Meghan was nothing. Against weaker mortals she acted the goddess but against one of her own, without the power of temptation, she wasn't so glib. When he didn't stop his advances, Meghan screeched in anger, lunging for him.

"Meghan!" Ian ordered, but it was too late.

"I should have been queen!" she yelled. "The throne was mine! I earned it."

Meghan bared her fangs, going for James' throat. He felt his brothers behind him. Rage poured from every inch in his body. The idea that she hurt Claudia made him see red. He didn't think, striking out to punch her in the face as she flew at him. Her head snapped and she flew backward, catching herself on all fours. Snarling, she attacked instantly.

"James," Roark began.

"She's mine," James growled. Meghan hit his face and they exchanged blows, crashing wildly around the room in a flurry of fang and claw. She scratched his arm, drawing blood as she gouged his flesh.

James didn't feel her punches. All he wanted was to take Meghan down. There was nowhere to run to, no one to rescue her and all her power and hatred were no match for what James felt for Claudia. An evil bitch like her could never understand what they had. His body became infused with the need to find Claudia, to save her, to avenge her if she were dead. The thought of Meghan claiming not just another victim but the carrier of his heart made him deadlier than he'd ever been in his life. Meghan might be strong but his love for Claudia was stronger.

On instinct, he caught Meghan's face as she came at him and broke her neck. She died instantly. Before her body hit the floor, he was outside, staring over the balcony. Narrowing his eyes, he tried to see down to the street. He detected far-off voices.

"Did you see that?" one woman asked.

"A dog just fell. I think someone pushed it," another said.

"That wasn't a dog. It was too big to be a dog," a man insisted. "I've never heard of a dog that big."

"Where'd it go?" the first woman asked.

James turned, hope filling him. Claudia could still be alive. "Her body isn't down there." He jogged toward the door. "But she might have shifted, running around the streets."

"We'll take care of this," Roark said, already dialing his phone. "Luckily, I have mob contacts here. I'm not proud of it but I have to admit it's good to have friends who can take care of bodies." Then throwing a pillow from the couch at James, he said, "Clean your face."

James caught the pillow and rubbed it hard across his features. When he pulled it back, the material was stained with blood.

"That'll do," Roark said.

"I'll take care of the hotel." Ian slipped out of his jacket and tossed it at James. "Looks like we'll have to use the newly signed musician who acted like a rock star excuse."

James nodded. His room door hung on the frame and Ian pushed it closed behind him. Not waiting for the elevators, he went to the stairwell. When he didn't hear anyone inside the steel column stairway, he leapt down the stairs, grabbing hold of the rail and swinging his body around so that he could speed down to the first floor. As he burst through the doors, it took all his willpower not to run suspiciously from the hotel. He pretended to check his watch, jog-running toward the beach-entrance doors at the back of the hotel as if he was late for an appointment. Outside, a crowd had gathered, still talking excitedly.

"It couldn't have fallen that far. Maybe a story, maybe two," a man said, sounding very sure of himself. "I'm sure it was just a Husky or Great Dane."

"Did you say Great Dane?" James asked, breathing hard from his run down forty-three flights.

"Yeah, your dog?" the man asked, scratching his balding head.

"No, clients. Damn guy signed a contract last

week and thinks he's already a rock star. Brought his girlfriend's dog and the stupid beast jumped out of the window. Seems he forgot to mention the thing likes to run." James mustered a smile he didn't feel through his worry.

"I don't think it was a Great Dane," a woman insisted. "I know dogs and that looked like a wolf of some sort."

"Mutt crossbreed," James said. She didn't look like she believed him. Turning back to the man, he asked, "Did you see which way it went?"

"That way," another woman said, pointing down toward the beach. "But the cops have already been called. They'll probably be out looking for it."

"I hope they find it," James lied, taking off down the beach, praying his story was convincing.

James lifted his nose to the sky. Within seconds, he detected her scent. Sprinting across the sandy shore, he neared the ocean and reached the hard, wet sand by the water. It didn't take him long to find paw prints in the sand. He wasn't surprised that she'd been called to the water. Though the moon wasn't full, the tides still listened to the celestial orb's commands.

"Claudia," he called, seeing a dark form near the waves. She turned to him, her body fully shifted into a beautiful female wolf. Her yellowed eyes narrowed and he felt her confusion and anger. Trying to link with his mind, he kept his thoughts gentle, *Easy, Claudia. I'm here to help you. I won't hurt you. I need you to trust me. It's over. Meghan's gone. She's dead and she won't hurt you or anyone else ever again. I promise you. It's over.*

She growled low in the back of her throat.

Claudia, I know you're confused. I'm confused. I don't know how you shifted before the first full moon, but you have. You're going to be all right. You're going to live. You've passed the final test of your turning.

She edged away from him, crouching low as the hair on her back stood up.

I'm sorry I didn't tell you about connecting to Meghan, but you have to believe me that's not why I took care of you.

Claim. The single word was a low, gravelly sound in his head.

James hesitated. Her body jerked as if she'd run and he hurried to answer. *Yes. I claimed you. I'm sorry I didn't tell you. But if you wish, you can be free of it. Breaking a claim isn't easy, but it can be done. It's not final. Nothing is final in the lycan world between a man and woman until we have the blessing of the king. Only then do we mate forever.*

Why? Again the single word punctured his thoughts.

Because... he hesitated.

Why? she demanded.

Because I love you. James took a deep breath. *Being with you is like... I can't explain it. I just love you, Claudia. I love you.*

Claudia shivered. James glanced around, sensing humans nearby. When he again looked at his love, she was on the sand, her body cracking and molding into her human form. She whimpered in pain as her body lengthened. Instantly, he was at her side, picking her up before she was fully turned.

"I love you too," she whispered, her eyes clear. "When Meghan and I met face-to-face, images became clearer. I don't think she meant to show me, but I saw her past. And then I fell and was sure I was dead, but the next thing I know I'm on this beach looking at you. I saw you kill her. It freed me from her thoughts, her evil."

"Are you sure you're not confused?" Hope welled up inside him and he was afraid of waking up from a dream.

"About you?" She pushed up, her naked body glorious in the moonlight. "I've known for a while. It wasn't clear but when you bit me, I felt you inside me. Besides," she gave a small smile, "I'm partially psychic."

He pulled her against him, kissing her soundly. Her warm mouth accepted him as easily as her heart. Every part of her invaded his senses and he opened his mind to her, letting her find whatever she wished of his soul. All he was belonged to her.

EPILOGUE

CLAUDIA SMILED, stretching her naked body as the sun rose over the mountain. The boards of the deck pressed into her back as the cool Rocky Mountain air caressed her breasts and stomach, tickling the thatch of hair between her thighs. Sensing James, she turned to see him standing in the window, holding two mugs of coffee. He wore a pair of denim jeans and nothing else. Unashamed of her nudity, she stood and walked inside.

"Good morning, beautiful. Have a good night?" James handed her a mug.

"Mmm," she moaned, suppressing a yawn. After Meghan's death, James had whisked her away. At first, they stayed with Roark and his wife Natasha until James finally managed to figure out where exactly he owned homes. She still couldn't imagine anyone losing track of real estate, but James had. Lucky for him, the clan bookkeepers hadn't. "Running with you through the forest by the light of the full moon always makes for a perfect evening."

"Hmm, I kind of thought the night before made for the perfect evening." He grinned and Claudia couldn't help but kiss him. Her breasts rubbed along his warm chest. Each day, she felt safer. James' love did that for her.

Meghan's body had been found mutilated like those of her previous victims. Her death was blamed on a serial killer, one who would unfortunately never be found. Though she had her reservations about it, Claudia knew they couldn't expose the lycan race and tell the world what really had happened.

"Want to make it a perfect morning?" She didn't break the full contact of their mouths.

"I would, but my family will be here soon."

"You finally figure out where you own a house and then you invite everyone over." She pouted her bottom lip.

"I thought you liked my family. Besides, we've had this place to ourselves for two months now." James nipped at her ear playfully. "And my father is bringing you a bunch of computer equipment so you can begin working again. Just like you asked."

"Yeah!" She gave a small cheer, clapping her hands. "Okay, they can come."

James laughed.

Claudia began walking toward their shared bedroom for clothes. Calling over her shoulder, she said, "Yes, I will marry you."

"I didn't ask."

She turned in the door, giggling at his shocked face. Her psychic gifts had increased, becoming stronger after each passing of the full moon. "You were going to." Winking, she turned to find some clothes. "And I say yes."

The End

ABOUT MICHELLE M. PILLOW

New York Times* & *USA TODAY
Bestselling Author

Michelle loves to travel and try new things, whether it's a paranormal investigation of an old Vaudeville Theatre or climbing Mayan temples in Belize. She believes life is an adventure fueled by copious amounts of coffee.

Newly relocated to the American South, Michelle is involved in various film and documentary projects with her talented director husband. She is mom to a fantastic artist. And she's managed by a dog and cat who make sure she's meeting her deadlines.

For the most part she can be found wearing pajama pants and working in her office. There may or may not be dancing. It's all part of the creative process.

Come say hello! Michelle loves talking with readers on social media!

www.MichellePillow.com

facebook.com/AuthorMichellePillow

twitter.com/michellepillow

instagram.com/michellempillow

bookbub.com/authors/michelle-m-pillow

goodreads.com/Michelle_Pillow

amazon.com/author/michellepillow

youtube.com/michellepillow

pinterest.com/michellepillow

COMPLIMENTARY EXCERPTS

TRY BEFORE YOU BUY!

Scientist Bridget Dutton has no time for traditional love. Her heart belongs to her work. Even though taking chemical readings of ocean water isn't her thing, she's willing to put in her time for her chance at exploring the Abyss. When her boat is attacked from below, Bridget's dream just might come true sooner than planned.

Caderyn the Hunter, the sexiest—and perhaps craziest—man she's ever laid eyes on may have rescued her from death, but who's going to rescue her from him? With a deliciously hot body and all the right moves, the man is a walking seduction that's too hard to resist. There's only one problem. Caderyn claims they're in the Abyss, living on a cursed island along the deep ocean floor. And, if that wasn't bad enough, he says he's a merman.

Sparks fly. Desires heat. But can Caderyn convince the logical Bridget there's room for more than one love in her heart?

🐾

Chapter One Extended Excerpt

Bridget Dutton watched the waves lapping along the bow of the ship as it chopped through the water. No matter how many times she went out to sea, she could never stop staring at the beauty of it—the brilliant blue of the water stretching like a moving field into the horizon. She loved everything about it—the sound, the smell, the feel of being rocked to sleep on the waves. But, there was also the excitement of it, the unknown.

Now, as the bright moonlight shimmered over the glassy surface, the water was exceptionally beautiful to behold. There was nothing around the boat except the sea and the night sky. They were miles away from any coast, surrounded by sparkling blue.

"Your mother must've thought she gave birth to a dolphin," Ned Devenpeck teased, joining her at the rail. He was the head of their expedition. His accent still held traces of his Dutch birth, but after nearly thirty years working off the Florida coast, primarily studying fish ecology, his English was perfect. Dev was an older man, nearing sixty, though he barely looked it. Years spent out on the waves had kept him fit and he hardly looked a day over thirty-five, except for the short crop of dark gray hair on his head. Like all the scientists, he was dressed for the field in khaki shorts and a fleece sweater. He handed her a cup of coffee. "You never come inside the cabin until it's time to sleep or work."

"Thanks, Dev," Bridget answered, nodding as she lifted the cup. She had known him for some time as a scientist, but she was beginning to think of him as a friend. This was their first expedition together, and he had chosen her as his second in command. There had been some light flirting, and she definitely respected his work, but it hadn't gone anywhere. She was only twenty-six and that was quite an age differ-ence, especially career wise. He was winding down while she was just getting started. "Actually, she accused me of being a pirate in my past life because I always came home with treasures from the ocean."

"Oh yeah? Where did you grow up?"

"The Oregon coast. Most of the treasures were

just sea shells or sand dollars, polished glass, bits of driftwood. But once, I did find this." Bridget reached into her shirt and pulled out her necklace. It was a flat disc with a hole in the middle inscribed with strange symbols. "No one has been able to tell me what it is or what it means. I've come to the conclusion that someone was toying with ancient languages and carved it. It's too new to be an antique."

Dev laughed softly. "I've never seen anything like it. And the Oregon coast? It's the wrong region for this sort of thing. Though, I suppose with currents... Well, never mind. It's probably like you said. So, is this the reason you love the ocean so much?"

"I don't know. It did make me think about it more, about what could be out there buried deep beneath the waves. I can't seem to help it. I love the sea. It's the last unknown left to explore on Earth. There are so many things we don't know about it. For each new species we classify, there are fifty more waiting around the next seamount."

"What are you doing in Florida, then?" Dev asked. "You should be going with a team to study the Mid-Atlantic Ridge or the effects of the Puerto Rico Trench on tsunamis. Why stay here helping me with boring chemical readings?"

"I tried to get on an expedition to explore shipwrecks, but Thurmond told me I lacked sufficient Deep Ocean and thermocline experience to be on his team. He did say if I filled this position and worked for a full year, he would reconsider my application. Since he's the boss, here I am."

"Thurmond's a politician first and a glory hound second," Dev said, shaking his head. "We're scientists. Politics have no place in science. Well, except to fund my pet projects, of course."

"I agree," Bridget said, raising her coffee mug. "But, don't you worry. I signed on to this boat for the next year, and I won't complain."

"I'm not worried," Dev said, winking. "We throw complainers to the sharks. There's no one for miles to aid in a rescue. How do you think we got rid of Grant?"

"Who's Grant?"

"Exactly." Dev winked again. He pushed up from the rail. "I'm tired. I'll see you in the morning."

Bridget laughed. "Good night."

"Don't stay up too late, kid. That's an order." Dev opened the door and went below deck into the main cabin.

Bridget smiled to herself as she turned back to the water. Hugging her sweater around her arms, she knew she shouldn't be out too much longer or she would catch cold. The air was particularly chilly at night, as the breeze swept over her from the water.

Just as she was about to turn, Bridget saw movement on the surface. She frowned, squinting to see more clearly. It was probably just a dolphin pod or something swimming past. She leaned over the rail. As the boat moved ahead, she saw that it was something floating on the water. She stiffened.

"Man overboard," she whispered. Where had he come from? Springing into action, she ran to the cabin door and yelled, "Man overboard! Man overboard!"

Someone was playing a guitar and the music came to a sudden halt, punctuated by the rise of voices. Nearly a dozen scientists rushed out from the cabin, some carrying life vests and first aid kits. Dev jumped up to man a searchlight as Bridget pointed at the water. It didn't take him long before he found the man clinging to driftwood. The big spotlight outlined the dark figure. Her stomach was tight with worry. Who was this man and what was he doing floating out in the middle of nowhere?

Bridget grabbed a rope ladder, still tied to the rail from earlier when they'd taken surface samples. She threw it over the side. Adrenaline pumped through her veins as she fearlessly climbed over the rail to the ladder. She didn't stop to think, just did what had to be done.

"Bridget, hold on!" she heard Cassandra scream. "Let us hand you a line so you can tie yourself off."

"We're close," Bridget yelled back. "I can almost reach him!"

The boat slowed. Freezing cold water splashed over her, soaking her sweater. She climbed down. Her feet dipped below the icy surface. Hooking her arm on a rung, she leaned over.

"Almost!" she called, beginning to shiver violently. "Just a foot more. Ease it in. I can almost... reach... him!"

The boat pulled closer. Her heart pounded so loudly in her ears that she couldn't hear anything. The man didn't move as she called out to him. His fingers gripped the driftwood for dear life. She reached out, touching his shirt sleeve. The man jerked, and she gasped in loud surprise at the sudden movement.

"What's going on?" she heard someone ask. The spotlight shifted, shining brightly into her eyes. She closed them, turning her back on the light as she gripped tighter to the man's sleeve.

"Easy, we're here to help. You're safe now,"

Bridget soothed. "No one's going to hurt you. Come on. Come with me. Easy does it. There you go."

The man started moving, grasping at her as he tried to pull himself out of the water. His heavier weight strained her arm on the rung. Bridget grunted in pain, trying to hold onto the man and the ladder. Calling up, she said, "I've got him, but I need help lifting him up."

Hands instantly came over the side to help her. Together they managed to get him up over the rail. Bridget stayed on the ladder, looking around. She climbed up a few rungs, getting her lower legs out of the freezing water.

"Are there any others?" she asked, coughing lightly. "Find out if there are any others."

"Bridget, come up," Dev yelled. "We're going to circle around the area."

Not seeing anyone in her immediate area, Bridget climbed up. Dev grabbed her under her arm and helped support her weight as she came over the top. Someone wrapped her shoulders in a wool blanket. The man she'd rescued was lying on the deck, covered by a blanket. She fell to her knees beside him. He was shivering, but his eyes were open.

Bridget tensed. His dark gaze stared up at her, and his black hair was matted to his head. The man was wearing an old fashioned linen ruff around his neck, an embroidered, padded epaulet, short stockings and puffed shorts much like those worn on the old Armada Galleons of the mid-fifteen hundreds. His skin was dark, though it was cast with a sick pallor. When he opened his mouth, a torrent of broken, foreign words passed his lips.

"Do you think he's from Cuba?" asked Stevens, a tall, lanky scientist who spent more time with a microscope than anyone she had ever known.

"Look at how he's dressed," someone whispered. "What's he doing out here?"

"Do you speak English?" Bridget asked him, when he continued in what sounded like a dialect of Spanish.

"Must go," he said, trying to sit up. His voice was hoarse making it even harder to understand his accent. He was too weak from his ordeal in the water and fell back to the deck. "Monsters. They're out there. In..."

"Monsters?" Dev asked, kneeling by Bridget. She shrugged, not understanding.

"It came from below," the man said. "A monster. It came from below. It rammed our ship."

"Military?" someone suggested.

"Monsters," the man insisted, desperately

grasping at Bridget's sweater. He pulled her down, shaking violently as his hand gripped into her sweater. "They come from below. They kill everyone. They control the water. They make it move."

Their ship bumped against something in the water. The man's eyes got wide and he began to cry, closing his eyes in what looked like prayer. Dev stood, and she heard him order, "You, man the spotlight and see what's out there. Everyone look for survivors. This man had to come from somewhere."

"It's too late," the man cried, before rushing into a torrent of broken Spanish. The ship again hit alongside something in the water. Bridget pulled her shirt free from the man's grip. "Too late. They kill us all."

"It's just driftwood," Dev yelled.

Bridget relaxed. Pointing at Stevens, she said, "Get him below deck and dried off. He's obviously in shock. See if you can't get a coherent thought out of him about what happened. Someone should get on the radio and try to find out what's going on. See if there are any missing ships, possibly some kind of movie set or reenactment crew."

"I've got the radio," Peterson answered. The bearded man turned to go below deck.

Bridget struggled to her feet, gripping the blanket tightly as she worked it snugly around her chest for warmth. Her bare legs and wet boots caused her muscles to ache with the extreme cold of the ocean breeze on her damp skin. She joined Dev by the railing as he searched the sea. The others had spread out and were searching with spotlights in all directions.

"What do you think happened?" Bridget asked, seeing chunks of wood floating around them.

"Shipwreck of some sort. There's too much debris in the water for this to just be a man lost at sea. I don't get it though. There are no reefs in this area to run aground on, unless he had been drifting for some time."

"But, if he's been drifting, then we wouldn't have this concentration of wood," Bridget said thoughtfully. "A storm maybe? A freak hurricane?"

"No," Dev denied easily. "The ocean's been calm and nothing has been picked up by our equipment. There haven't been any major storms for weeks. And if there were anything unusual, our satellite uplink would have warned us of it."

"Do you think he meant sharks, not monsters? His English wasn't the best." Bridget searched the water. More debris floated by. Her stomach knotted. She couldn't see any more survivors. "They wouldn't have attacked a boat, but if there were blood in the water... I don't know, maybe it's possible?"

"Yes, possible," Dev answered. He pointed into the distance. "There. What's that?" Then glancing over his shoulders, he called, "I need a spotlight over here."

Light skimmed the dark ocean surface. The debris grew thicker, clanking along the boat. Bridget shivered. "It's been torn up. What in the world could have caused this much damage? There's nothing out here but water."

"It's wood," Dev said, his tone strained, "All of it wood. And did you see what he was wearing? This doesn't make sense."

"Film crew? Maybe the pyrotechnics went awry." Bridget frowned. So far it was the only idea she had that sounded reasonable given the facts.

"No, they would've had backup ships for everyone." Dev turned. "Tom, tell Jon to check our bearings. I want to make sure we haven't drifted off course. Check the sensors and make sure there are no reefs around this area." Dev visibly swallowed. "Everyone else, keep searching for survivors. With this much wood, the ship was way too big for just one man."

For a long time everyone was quiet, as they

looked through the floating debris, listening past the sound of wood bumping the sides of the fiberglass ship. A blast from the horn sounded over the water, much louder than any yell. They listened to the silence that followed the abrasive noise. Time crept by slowly and no one called out in answer.

"There," Tom said to her left. Two divers were in full gear, ready to go into the water. "What is that? Do you see it?"

They watched as a sail snagged on a broken beam drifted by. A wrist had tangled on the mast, but the rest of the body was below the surface. Dev sent the divers into the water to see if the person was still alive. Though, when they dragged the body of a man out of the water, they were not surprised that he was long dead. He was dressed much like the first strange man now below deck.

"See if he has any ID and then wrap him in a blanket," Dev said softly. Bridget heard him whisper under his breath, "Poor souls."

Bridget rubbed her eyes. They'd had a long day at sea collecting samples, but they weren't tired as they focused on the endless ocean and their new rescue mission.

"You should get changed from those wet clothes,"

Dev said. "I don't need you getting sick on me way out here."

Bridget nodded and gave one last glance over the water before going below deck to the female sleeping quarters. The quarters consisted of several cots lined along the walls. As there were more males than females aboard the ship, they had more room in their quarters than the men had. Changing out of her wet clothes into warmer blue jeans and a thick hooded sweatshirt, she quickly pulled the bun from the nape of her neck, only to wind her long hair up. When she finished, a strand of her black hair clung to her pale hands. Her fingers shook, and she clenched them into a fist, wiping the hair strand against her jeans.

Death at sea was a risk they all took on the water. The ocean wasn't something they'd ever be able to control. Even as she admired it, the reality of what it could do humbled her. Bridget heard the cries of the survivor, though he again spoke in his native tongue. He sounded so terrified. Bridget wanted to go to him, but knew her help was needed on the deck. She made her way topside.

Two more bodies were pulled from the wreckage, but there were no more survivors. Each corpse only added to the mystery, as the men were all dressed in the same period costume, and the only papers they found were handwritten parchments in a foreign language. Only a few words could be made out, as the water had caused most of the ink to run.

Still, after an hour passed without any luck, no one suggested giving up the search. Jon was having a hard time getting anyone on the radio, but insisted that they were still on course. Steven reported that the survivor was asleep. They'd given him a shot of morphine from the emergency medical kit to put him out since he wouldn't calm down.

They crossed through the thickest part of the debris before circling around. The horn sounded intermittently over their heads. Aside from the debris, there was no sign of a ship, making them believe that it had been alone on the water before it had sunk.

Bridget closed her eyes briefly, taking a deep breath. The salty air stung her face, and she drew the hood of her sweatshirt over her head. Suddenly, the ship rocked, hit on the starboard side. A loud crash punctuated the startled screams of those onboard. The boat tilted so violently that she fell over, slamming into the deck. Several of the scientists slid into each other as the ship righted itself once more.

Bridget hung onto the rail, pulling herself up. Her body tense, she searched desperately to see what it was that had hit them. The boat tipped again, this time knocked from the port side. Several screams sounded, louder than before. One of the scientists fell overboard into the dark water.

"Where is he?" Stevens yelled. "Jerry?!"

Bridget was about to go and help when the boat was hit again. She saw a strange glimmer in the water, a brief passing of silvery blue light. Dev grabbed her arm as they were again tossed, keeping her from falling over the side like Jerry.

"We got him," Stevens said as they pulled Jerry back up from the water.

"Submarine?" Bridget asked Dev, pointing to where she'd seen the glimmer. They were scientists and would look for the most logical answer first. Another flash passed by, this one silvery green. "Did you see that?"

"I've never seen a sub move like that," Dev answered, "not even the small submersibles."

"Aliens?" someone asked, pointing to another glimmer of light.

Bridget gripped the rail as they were again knocked on the starboard. "New, colossal species of Deep Ocean fish rising to the surface to feed?"

"I'll go with that one," Dev announced. "Someone get me the net and a harpoon. We're going to try and catch this thing. Let's see what we're up against, shall we? Come on now! Move it, people!"

Dev clapped his hands. The scientists sprang into action. Some scrambled down to the cabin. Whatever was knocking the boat had stopped. Those left on deck looked over the side, trying to see anything that would give them a clue as to what was happening. Stevens got Jerry below deck and to safety.

"I wish we had a submersible," Dev said. Bridget nodded. They hadn't had a reason to take one on this trip. "We could stick it down there with a video feed and use it as a decoy."

The ocean was calm once more for several minutes. Stevens directed the men to drop the net down into the water as Dev waited with his harpoon. Bridget watched, her body tense.

"Should we really kill it?" Bridget asked, always the scientist first.

"We may not have a choice," Dev said, though she could tell by his face that he would love to catch the thing alive. "You saw what it did to that other ship."

Bridget nodded. He was right, of course. A strange blend of scientific excitement and mortal fear beat in her veins. She held her breath, waiting.

The water stirred. A palpable tension worked its way over the deck as they all watched the net. It dipped into the cold water, jerking violently as it caught hold of something. Stevens ordered it pulled up. As it neared the surface, Bridget saw the purplish glimmer of diamond shaped scales and the splash of a long split caudal fin. The way it moved reminded her of silk in water. It was larger than any fish she'd ever heard of. A long, short dorsal fin ran up the back, but she couldn't see the fish's head. Then a male arm thrust up from the water. They all gasped in shock as the fingers moved.

"He's still alive," Stevens said, though none of them knew who the 'he' was. "That thing is swallowing him whole."

The way the body was angled, it did look as if the fish had swallowed half the man's body, starting at the feet. The men pulled the net harder, grunting in their efforts, but the sea creature and his victim didn't surface. Then, the body shifted and Bridget gasped. By the way the scales blended into flesh, it didn't look like a man at all.

"Merman," Bridget whispered, trying desperately to see into the dark water. Such a discovery would be phenomenal. "Give us a better spotlight over here!"

"Shoot it, Dev," Stevens yelled.

Dev leveled the harpoon. The ship rocked violently, throwing off his aim, and he nicked the creature's tail. Bridget saw the merman's blood seconds before the net was jerked up, empty. It had been cut open and the creature freed.

Bridget yelled as she was thrown across the deck. The sound of the ship breaking apart beneath them pierced the night. Several of the scientists slid into the water. Bridget's eyes met Cassandra's before the woman went over the side. Bridget had never really gotten along with the woman, but it didn't stop her from reaching out to grab at her arm. Cassandra's fingers slipped through her grasp. The boat jerked again, coming apart in a way that should not have been possible. Water splashed over the edges. They were sinking, fast.

Bridget screamed. Then, as the first shock of cold water hit her skin, she took a deep breath, tears streaming over her cheeks as she held it. Time seemed to stand still as she sank slowly down into the black water. The pull of the sinking boat tugged her body as she went under the surface. She flailed her arms, trying to swim against the current that was dragging her down.

Her lungs burned, even as the cold seeped into

her limbs. Within seconds, she couldn't move. It was a dark, soundless, watery tomb. She couldn't hear the struggles of the others. She couldn't hear the creaking ship. Then, a small glimmer of light appeared before her. Was she dying? Was this it? The light faded as her mind dimmed.

One last thought passed over her before she let the darkness have her. *Monsters. They came from below.*

To find out more about Michelle's books visit www.MichellePillow.com

THE SAVAGE KING

BY MICHELLE M. PILLOW

Lords of the Var® Book One by Michelle M. Pillow

Bestselling Cat-shifter Romance Series

Cat-shifting King Kirill knows he must do his duty by his people. When his father unexpectedly dies, it's his destiny to take the throne and all of the responsibility that entails. What he hadn't prepared for is the troublesome prisoner that's now his to deal with.

Undercover Agent Ulyssa is no man's captive. Trapped in a primitive forest awaiting pickup, she's going to make the best out of a bad situation...which doesn't include falling for the seductions of a king.

❧

About *Lords of the Var*® (Books 1-5)

You met their father, King Attor, in Dragon Lords Books 1-4, now meet the Var Princes!

The cat-shifter princes were raised to not believe in love, especially love for one woman, and they will do everything in their power to live up to their father's expectations. Oh, how the mighty will fall.

🐾

The Savage King Excerpt

Kirill watched the door to his bedroom open. He'd been sitting in the dark, trying to relieve the stress headache that had built behind his eyes for the last week. The pain started at the base of his skull and radiated up to his temples until he could hardly see straight.

A heavy responsibility had been thrust on his shoulders, a responsibility he really hadn't prepared himself for, the welfare of the Var people. King Attor had not left him in a good position. He'd rallied the people to the brink of war, convinced them that the Draig were their enemy, and even went so far as to attack the Draig royal family.

Kirill wanted to see peace in the land. However, he knew the facts didn't bode well for it. The Draig had a long list of grievances against King Attor and the Var kingdom.

Before his death, the king had ordered an attack on the four Draig princes, all of which ended horribly for the Var. The worst was when Prince Yusef was stabbed in the back, a most cowardly embarrassment for the Var guard who did it. If he hadn't been executed in the Draig prisons, he would've been ostracized from the Var community. Luckily, Prince Yusef survived or they'd already be at battle.

Attor had also arranged for the kidnapping of Yusef's new bride. The Draig Princess Olena had been rescued, or that too would've led to war. The old king had even tried to poison Princess Morrigan, the future Draig queen, on two separate occasions. She too lived. And those were only a few of the offenses Kirill knew about in the few weeks before King Attor's death. He could just imagine what he didn't know.

Kirill sighed, feeling very tired. He'd known since birth that the day would come when he'd be expected to step up and lead the Var as their new king. He just hadn't expected it to be for another hundred or so years. His father had been a hard man, whom he'd foolishly believed was invincible.

"Here kitty, kitty, kitty." His lovely houseguest's whisper drew his complete attention from his heavy thoughts.

Ulyssa bent over like she expected him to answer to the insulting call. He dropped his fingers from his temple into his lap, and a quizzical smile came to his lips. As he watched her, he wasn't sure if he was angered or amused by her words.

"Are you in here, you little furball?" she said, a little louder.

She wore his clothes. Never had the outfit looked sexier. His jaw tightened in masculine interest, as he unabashedly looked her over. All too well did he remember the softness of her body against his and the gentle, offering pleasure of her sweet lips. She'd made soft whimpering noises when he'd touched her, yielding, purring sounds in the back of her throat. Even with the aid of nef, he was surprised by how easily and confidently she melted into him. The Var were wild, passionate people and were drawn to the same qualities in others. He suspected she'd be an untamed lover.

Too bad she'd belonged to his father first. In his mind, that made her completely untouchable though none would dare question his claim if he were to take her to his bed. Technically, by Var law, she belonged to him until he chose to release her. For an insane moment, he thought about keeping her as a lover. He knew he wouldn't, but the thought was entertaining.

Kirill's grin deepened. Ulyssa strode across his home to the bathroom door with an irritated scowl. It was obvious she didn't see him in the darkened corner, watching her. He detected her engaging smell from across the room, the smell of a woman's desire. It stirred his blood, making his limbs heavy with arousal. And, for the first time since his father's death, his headache relieved itself.

"Hum, maybe I'm looking too high. I'm sure there has to be a little cat door here somewhere. Come here, little kitty. Where are you hiding?"

His slight smile fell at her words. It was easy to detect her mocking tone.

"Where's your little kitty door, huh?" Ulyssa whispered to herself, her blue gaze searching around in the dark.

Kirill grimaced in further displeasure. He watched her open the door to his weapons cabinet. Her eyes rounded, and he thought she might take one. She didn't. Instead, she nodded in appreciation before closing the door and continuing her search for an exit.

She stopped at a narrow window by his kitchen doorway. Her neck craned to the side, as she tried to see out over the distance. Kirill knew she looked at the forest. From under her breath, he heard her vehement whisper, "Where exactly did you little fur balls bring me? Ugh, I need to get out of this flea trap, even if I have to fight every one of you cowardly felines to do it. I've fought species twice as big and three times as frightening. A couple of little kitty cats don't scare me."

If this insolent woman wanted to play tough, oh, he'd play. Curling gracefully forward, Kirill shifted before his hands even touched the ground. He let one thick paw land silently on the floor, followed by a second. Short black fur rippled over his tanned flesh, blending him into the shadows. His clothes fell from his body, and he lowered his head as he crept forward. A low sound of warning started in the back of his throat. He was livid.

To find out more about Michelle's books visit www.MichellePillow.com

PLEASE LEAVE A REVIEW

THANK YOU FOR READING!

Please take a moment to share your thoughts by
reviewing this book.

Be sure to check out Michelle's other titles at

www.MichellePillow.com

www.ingramcontent.com/pod-product-compliance
Lightning Source LLC
Chambersburg PA
CBHW030629120726
47904CB00006B/2090